Emmerdale Farm Book 16

The Homecoming

'May I speak to Mr Skilbeck?' asked a calm, crisp voice. 'This is Dr Kinsa of Bradford General Hospital.'

'I'll fetch him,' Annie said, and ran with pounding heart to the cow parlour.

Matt turned as she approached. One look at her face and he didn't wait to hear her words. He was gone in a moment. Annie stepped into the gap Matt had left and she and Joe got on with finishing the milking. Matt came out, changed out of his white coat and boots. He was pulling on his jacket.

'They want me there at once,' he said. 'Dolly's taken a turn for the worse.'

Available in Fontana by the same author

Emmerdale Farm Book 12: Face Value
Emmerdale Farm Book 13: Good Neighbours
Emmerdale Farm Book 14: Innocent Victim
Emmerdale Farm Book 17: Old Flames
Emmerdale Farm Book 19: Family Feuds
Emmerdale Farm Book 20: Young Passions

LEE MACKENZIE

The Homecoming

Emmerdale Farm Book 16

Based on the successful
Yorkshire Television series
originated by Kevin Laffan

FONTANA/Collins

First published by Fontana Paperbacks 1982
Fourth impression April 1986

Made and printed in Great Britain by
William Collins Sons & Co Ltd, Glasgow

Chapter One

When the ambulance siren was heard in Beckindale, heads turned, conversations were interrupted. Henry Wilks went to the window of the Woolpack and saw it manoeuvre round two hesitating cars at the Beck Bridge, then forge on at full speed through the High Street towards the fork in the road.

'Someone's in trouble,' he said as he moved back into the back premises of the inn.

'Where was it going?'

'Can't be sure.' Henry paused. 'It might have been going up to Emmerdale, Amos.'

His partner looked down at the cutlery he was drying. 'Hope nowt's wrong wi' Dolly,' he muttered.

Amos Brearly would have been the last man in the world to make a song and dance about it, but the fact was, he was very fond of Dolly Skilbeck. Much though he hated having female persons in the living quarters of the pub, he made an exception in Dolly's case. She had lightened up the place while she worked there, had learned how to handle her employer's quirky nature. He had even taken a hand, though no one but Annie Sugden knew it, in furthering Dolly's love affair with Matt.

Now she was expecting a baby, was around two months pregnant. Amos could never bring himself to discuss such things as pregnancy; the nearest he came to it was murmuring that Dolly was in a 'delicate condition'. He had watched her with anxiety these last few days, and seen how poorly she looked.

But the ambulance couldn't be for Dolly. She was a healthy lass, and there was no reason in the world why anything should go wrong with the dearly-awaited baby.

This was more or less what Dr Alexander had told the family at Emmerdale. 'She'll be all right,' she said. 'Infection of this kind isn't uncommon in the early months and she's a healthy young woman. But for the course of antibiotics she needs, hospital is best.' She didn't mention that the first three months of pregnancy were the most dangerous, and that Dolly was best in hospital if anything was to prove really serious.

Matt had gone with Dolly in the ambulance. Annie Sugden moved about the farmhouse kitchen, busying herself with the usual chores of the morning. 'She should never have tried to get up this morning,' she sighed. 'The minute she came downstairs, I knew . . .'

'Well, you did the right thing to call me, and we've got her off to Hotten at once. Don't you worry about it, Mrs Sugden. Hotten Cottage Hospital is well able to deal with a thing like this.'

But before the day was out, the news came that Dolly had had to be transferred to an intensive care unit in Bradford. Matt had gone with her. He came home in the evening looking haggard. 'They say there's nowt to be done for t'moment,' he reported. 'They're giving her injections and one thing and another.' His voice faltered. She had looked so unlike herself, so small and frail under the sheets with all the frightening equipment hooked up to her.

'What's to do, then?' Sam Pearson enquired. 'Can we go and visit her tomorrow?'

That he should even envisage making the trip to Bradford was a token of the old man's anxiety. Matt shook his head at him. 'Nay, Grandad, she's not having visitors for the present.'

Joe had gone to Demdyke, but rang from the box in the village about an hour later. 'What's the news, Ma?' he asked with muted apprehension.

'It's not good, lad,' his mother replied, with a glance over her shoulder to make sure her father was sleeping in his chair. 'Matt's upstairs having a lie-down. He looked worn out when he got back. Dolly's gone to Bradford General for special treatment. From the way Matt describes it, I think she's on a drip.'

Joe gave a whistle of dismay. 'Bad as that?'

'These things happen, Joe. It's some germ . . . But they can do wonders these days with their drugs an' all.'

'But how did she get it? I mean, granted a farm's a mucky place – '

'Oh, it's nowt to do with that, lad. It's quite a different kind of germ. Dr Alexander seemed to think . . .' She let the words die. She'd been going to say, Dr Alexander seems to think it may have something to do with poor care after her first pregnancy. But no one else except herself and Matt knew that Dolly had had an illegitimate baby years ago, and no one needed to know now. 'She seemed to think that it was something the hospitals are quite used to in pregnant women,' she amended. 'Any road, Matt's been told t'best thing is to let them get on with the treatment and come back in the morning.'

'Shall I tell Henry and Amos?' Joe asked. 'It's funny, Amos is like a cat on hot bricks about her.'

'Just tell them she's gone to Bradford for some special care,' Annie said.

'Aye.' Knowing his money was about to run out, Joe added quickly: 'Ma, if Dolly loses that baby, it'll break her in pieces.'

'There's no question of that, Joe.' Not yet, she thought, as she hung up.

Matt was up and about as usual next morning when Annie rose, prepared to go out to meet Joe in the mistle. 'Matt! Why didn't you take a lie-in?'

'I've been awake for ages, Ma. Seemed best to get up and get on with it.'

'Nay, lad, I'll do your stint – '

He shook his head. 'What d'you want me to do – hang about in here waiting for t'phone to ring?'

She studied him. His round face, usually so fresh and pink, was wan. There were shadows under the frank, honest eyes. She realized that though he was physically tired, he wouldn't sit down and rest. He needed to be kept busy. She sighed and took off the cardigan she'd put on for the coolness of the mistle at this early-morning hour. 'Right, then, lad, off you go,' she agreed.

She was putting bacon and sausages into the Aga's oven to keep warm when the phone rang. She glanced at the fine old wall clock. Seven-fifteen. To be rung so early in the morning augured anything but well. She hastened to the phone. Her father, moving about upstairs getting dressed, came to the landing to listen.

'May I speak to Mr Skilbeck?' asked a calm, crisp voice. 'This is Dr Kinsa, of Bradford General.'

'I'll fetch him,' she said, put the receiver down on the dresser, and ran with pounding heart to the cow parlour.

Matt turned as she approached. One look at her face and he didn't have to hear her words. He took his hands away from the valves he was regulating on the container-tank, and was gone in a moment. Joe looked at Annie. 'Hospital?'

'Aye.'

'Oh, lord!' But they said no more for the moment. Annie stepped into the gap Matt had left, and between them they got on with finishing up the morning's milking. Matt came out while they were turning on the water to hose out.

He had changed out of his white coat and boots. He was pulling on his jacket. 'They want me there at once,' he said. 'She's taken a turn for the worse.'

'Do you want me to come with you?' Annie asked quickly.

'Nay, it'd only delay me.' It wasn't meant unkindly, and she took no offence.

'Take my car – '

'Aye, thanks.' He showed her the keys, already in his hand. 'I'll ring as soon as I can.'

'Aye. Off with you, then.'

Sam Pearson was sitting in his chair as Annie went into the kitchen. 'I heard the end of it,' he explained as his daughter came in. 'They seemed to think it was awful urgent to get him there.'

'Well, Dad, there's lots of urgencies in having a baby.'

'But not at this stage, Annie.'

'No,' she agreed. She had taken off her shoes at the door and now went upstairs to put on others. When she came down Joe had come in. She served breakfast. No one said much. All their thoughts were fixed on Matt and his journey to the hospital.

Dr Kinsa proved to be an Indian of about thirty-five. He

greeted Matt with brisk calmness. 'I'm afraid things have not gone well, Mr Skilbeck. The infection didn't respond to the early course of antibiotics.'

'What does that mean, doctor?' Matt said.

Dr Kinsa put his hand on Matt's sleeve. 'The child is already dead, I'm afraid. That means – '

'I know what it means,' Matt said.

'We have to operate,' the doctor said. 'At once. Have we your permission?'

'Of course.' He hesitated, looking down at the slim brown hand on his sleeve. 'She's going to be all right?'

The doctor waited till he looked up to meet his gaze. 'We hope so, Mr Skilbeck, we hope so.'

They showed him to a room where he could wait until the operation was completed. He found a pay-phone and rang home. He explained that the baby was lost, no hope at all in that respect, and that it seemed they wouldn't know for some days after the operation whether they could check the infection that had wrecked the pregnancy. 'I'll let you know as soon as she comes out of theatre,' he said.

'I'm coming to the hospital, Matt,' Annie said.

Joe drove her in the Land-Rover. But traffic was heavy and by the time they got there, the patient was in the recovery room. 'As well as can be expected,' the surgeon told Matt.

Annie sat down to wait with him until Dolly should regain consciousness. Joe had to get back to the farm but left with great reluctance.

He thought about Ed Hathersage as he drove back. Ed had come from the United States to claim his inheritance, the farm that had belonged to old Hathersage, and had found a new interest in farming during his stay in Beckindale. For a time he'd even imagined himself settling in the house of his great-uncle, running the farm. Good sense had prevailed and he'd left the farmhouse and a small stretch of land for a 'living museum', while selling a few acres to Joe to finance the project. But on getting back to Kansas, Ed had found his life as a trailer-camp operator beyond endurance. Much to Joe's surprise he'd got an enthusiastic letter from Ed, explaining how he'd sold up and bought a stretch in Dakota on which he intended to take up the life of his forebears, farming folk all.

But before he did so, Ed wanted to take a look at how farms were run in that state and neighbouring states. He'd actually invited Joe to come out and stay with him for a while. 'All you need is your air fare – I'll put you up and pay for transportation when we start travelling,' Ed had written. 'Come on, why don't you come? You might learn a lot from looking at American farming methods.'

So he might, indeed. And even to get away, to go there and see something fresh, something optimistic and forward-looking . . . Not that there was any chance of that. Plans like that took capital and a lot more room than Joe had at his disposal. Henry would co-operate on the money side if he thought it a good investment, but even Henry couldn't provide more land at a cheap rate.

So Joe felt doomed to go on in the same way as for generations: up at the crack of dawn, work finished at nightfall or, at harvest time, when the last acre had been cleared. Day in, day out, almost without remission. They hadn't enough staff to allow much in the way of holidays. Why, with Matt away, they had to call in temporary help. It was all wrong. There ought to be a better way of doing things.

Perhaps if he took up Ed's invitation to the States he'd find that better way. But there was no chance of going. Who would step into his shoes if he went? It would mean hiring on someone for a month or two, and although they could afford it, the expense was hard to justify. Henry would be the first to say the money could be better spent, although he wouldn't stand in Joe's way. But Joe would feel guilty about it.

No, it was out of the question. Having reduced himself to a state of complete depression about his own poor prospects and the anxiety about Dolly, Joe drove back to the farm to get on with the day's work.

Judy Westrop, coming out of the village stores, was just too late to catch his eye and stop him. She'd have liked to have a word with him. Her excuse would have been to enquire after Dolly's condition but the truth was, it always helped her to chat with Joe. He had been a big factor in helping her to get treatment for her incipient alcoholism; shame at having embarrassed him on the first occasion when they went out together had made her face the fact that she was messing up her life.

He had never mentioned that evening to her. When she'd tried to apologize he cut her short with: 'Heck, Judy, if we all went back over the mistakes we've made, we'd never have time for normal conversation! Just forget it.'

But she never would, nor how he had taken her home to Emmerdale rather than unload on to her father this unconscious female child who was making his situation in Beckindale a mortification. Partly as a result of Joe's calm goodwill, she had decided to go for treatment at a clinic.

Judy had come back to Beckindale determined to make herself part of the community. She wasn't going to go back to textile engineering; city life was too obsessed with fashion and keeping up with the Joneses, relationships tended to be casual and, in the circles in which she had moved, too much connected with getting promotion. Beckindale was the absolute opposite; here life moved at an easy, gentle pace. Friendships once formed were permanent. That didn't mean people were all loving-kindness – by no means, passions could be as fierce here as anywhere. But at least relationships weren't built up with the intention of cutting them short the moment it became convenient to do so. She wanted to make herself part of Beckindale.

And perhaps to make herself important to Joe Sugden, too.

When Joe came indoors, his grandfather was moving about the kitchen in a sort of agitated march. 'That confounded thing!' he roared, pointing a shaking finger at the telephone. 'Keeps ringing, and I can't get any sense out of it when I pick it up!'

'What?' Joe said. 'How'd you mean?'

'It rang three times – no, four – and there was a funny hissing noise and some clanks and clicks. Once there was somebody yattering away – some foreign rubbish.'

'Foreign?' Joe's mind did a quick double-take. 'Italian?'

'Eh? You what?' Sam sank down suddenly on a kitchen chair. 'I never thought of that,' he said.

'Did you give the number when you replied?'

'Didn't pick it up the last twice,' Sam grunted, going red with vexation.

Joe sighed inwardly. His grandfather would never come to terms with the telephone. When he was forced to answer it, he tended to pick it up and roar: 'Yes? What d'you want?' which wasn't an encouraging opening to any conversation.

'Well, I've got to get on,' he said. 'If it rings again, think on – it's probably Jack calling from Rome.'

'Aye . . . well . . . I'll see . . .'

This didn't augur well for any contacts between Emmerdale and Rome; but at that moment the phone rang again. Joe picked it up, watched keenly by the old man. True enough, there were funny noises on the line, but Joe persisted in announcing that this was Emmerdale Farm and giving the number, until at length a girl's voice said: '*Rimanete all'apparecchio!*' then '*Pronto!*' and with a final click Jack Sugden came on, loud and clear.

'Joe? That you? I've had the devil of a time getting through.'

'Aye . . . well . . . Never mind about that. What's to do?'

'Listen, Joe, is Ma there?'

'No, she's at the hospital.'

'Hospital?' There was immediate alarm in his brother's voice. Parted by many miles and some years of neglect, his mother still meant a lot to Jack Sugden.

'She's not ill, it's Dolly. Summat to do with the baby. Ma went to be with Matt while they do an operation.'

'An operation! That sounds bad – what's wrong, Joe?'

'Dunno. Seems she's losing the baby, that's all I can gather. Any road, Ma and Matt are at the hospital waiting for her to come round from the anaesthetic. I just dropped Ma there and rushed back. We're in a bit of a state here, Jack – I'm the only worker on the job at the moment.' He didn't actually add, 'So what are you wasting my time for, keeping me chatting on the phone,' but there was something of that in his manner. Joe could easily be irritated by Jack's assumption that they would all huddle round the phone and wait to talk to him when he chose to ring.

'Right, I get the point,' Jack said without taking offence. 'Will you tell Ma when she gets back that I'm coming home?'

'Home?'

'Aye, to Emmerdale.'

'When?'

'Any minute now. Expect me when you see me.'

'What?' Joe gasped. 'Bit sudden, isn't it?'

'Well, you know me, lad – he who hesitates is lost, that's my motto. Once I make up my mind, I get on with it.'

More like 'Once I make up my mind, I don't know what I've made it up to', Joe thought. His brother was a strange, impulsive creature, almost the exact opposite of Joe in many respects. Joe had a natural instinct for the business of farming which experience had improved until now he weighed up everything he did without knowing he did so. Very rarely did he give way to impulse. Experience had taught him to keep himself in check. He'd made two bad mistakes in his life; his marriage, and his relationship with Kathy. Both were in the personal domain. In things like deciding where to live and where to invest, he was canny beyond his years.

'Will you be staying long?' he enquired of Jack.

'Depends.'

'On what?'

'I'll explain it all when I see you. It's okay to come, isn't it? I mean, you can put me up?'

'Of course.' There was the room Matt used to occupy, kept now as a spare room after Matt and Dolly had converted the attic into a little bedsitter for themselves. Jack knew this perfectly well. He was just going through the motions of making sure his younger brother would welcome him home. To do him justice, Jack was always careful to give Joe his due at Emmerdale. Joe was the boss, though he was the younger brother. Jack understood that.

'Righto then – you'll tell Ma? I'll try to ring again to let her know – '

Sam, who had been hovering in the background picking up most of this conversation, barked in Joe's ear: 'Tell him to bring some seeds of courgettes, Joe! Them Italian courgettes is first rate. Tell him to – '

'Grandad, hang on a minute! We're trying to arrange – '

'I heard that,' Jack interrupted, laughing. 'Okay, I'll try to remember to buy some courgette seeds before I take off. 'Bye, Joe.'

'Wait a minute, I – '

But the connection had been broken. Joe understood perfectly. Jack didn't want to discuss his decision. For a man whose business was words, Jack was very poor at using them in face-to-face situations with other members of the human race. Reticent to the point of secretiveness, Jack never told anyone anything about himself unless he had to. Even now, Joe didn't know the ins and outs of his brother's first leaving home and becoming a writer.

His life in Rome was more accessible, in a way. After the success of his novel, *Field of Tares*, Jack had gone to Rome to write the script for the film and had won a prize for it. The sexiness of the book, the sexiness of the film and the actresses who took part in it, various attentions from the *papparazzi* in Italy and gossip writers in *Der Stern* had made Jack Sugden something of an international celebrity.

All of a sudden he was coming home.

One thing was certain. He couldn't be coming at a better time. Ma was really upset about Dolly and the baby. The news of Jack's impending visit would cheer her up tremendously.

Sam wanted the whole conversation repeated to him, though he'd got a good idea of the gist of it. Then he wanted the latest news about Dolly. 'Dunno how long Ma will be staying there,' Joe said. 'Can I leave it to you to get summat together for a meal at midday, Grandad?'

'Aye, I'll see to it, lad.' Sam could always be relied on when it came to a crunch. Crusty and wayward he might be from time to time, but when he was needed he would never fall short. 'Shall I make you a cupper now, before you go out?'

'Better not, Grandad. There's them ewes of Matt to see to,

and feed to shift into the mistle, and t'vet's coming to look at Campion.'

'Tell you what, I'll bring it out to you at the fold – '

'Righto. And if the phone rings again, Grandad, say the number when you pick it up, eh?'

When Joe had gone out Sam put the kettle on and warmed the pot. He had just put the tea cosy over it and was taking the vacuum flask out of the cupboard when there was a tap on the door and Seth Armstrong came in.

'What you doing here, Seth?' Sam demanded, annoyed at being caught in the midst of domestic activity.

'First off, I came to enquire after t'lass. How's she doing?'

'Not good, Seth. Matt and Annie are waiting at the hospital now to see how she came through the operation.'

Seth clicked his large teeth in sympathy. 'Poor child. Why should it happen to her, that so sorely wanted a babby? While some silly kid that couldn't care less can have childer one after t'other, no problem.' Seth sighed, pulled at his droopy black moustache, and eyed the tea cosy. 'If that's fresh tea, Sam, I wouldn't mind a cup.'

'You'll have to wait, then. I'm taking it out to Joe first. There's just the two of us for the moment, to run the place.'

'I'll take it out to him, Sam, if you'll pour a cup ready for when I come back.'

Sam took up the offer, not without some consideration of what Seth was up to now. One thing you could be sure of with Seth, when he came to see you there was always an ulterior motive.

It came out when the two men were settled by the table with cups of tea and Annie's parkin biscuits on a plate between them. 'Amos is right bothered about t'lass,' Seth mused, crunching with his strong, tombstone teeth.

'So we all are.'

'Aye, but I'd like to do summat to cheer Amos up.'

'Would you?' Sam said, looking at Seth with suspicion.

'He's always wanted an allotment, hasn't he?'

'We-ell . . .' In the flush of first discovering the wholefood way of life and the benefits of fresh salads, Amos had made Henry's life a misery with grated carrot, marrow stuffed with breadcrumbs and herbs, and natural yoghourt. Along with this had gone a regret, often stated, that he had nowhere to plant a few seeds. It was hopeless to try digging up the plot at the back of the Woolpack – it was often needed for the storage of extra crates of soft drinks in the summer, and Amos dried his glass cloths and such of his laundry as he thought fit for public display on a line out there.

So he had, in fact, applied for an allotment. But there was a waiting list. Despite the fact that Beckindale was a country community, few of the houses in the village had large gardens. Many of them opened straight on to the street, but had a stretch of ground at the back – but not large enough for both flowers and vegetables. So many Beckindalers had allotments too, or had been waiting on the list ahead of Amos.

'D'you think he really means it?' Seth went on. 'I mean, it wasn't just talk?'

'No, I think he was serious,' Sam admitted. He rubbed his forehead and the expanse of scalp that went back into his sparse grey hair. 'You saying there's one available?'

'I got a pal on the management committee of the Allotment Society,' Seth said. This wasn't surprising. Seth had friends everywhere. 'He says there's one come free, but thing is, there's two folk who might get it – one's Amos, t'other's Stuart Gommell, lives over by Peck Lane. But I hear he's thinking of moving to Scarborough, to work in a boarding-house there. Know if it's true?'

'Could be. He can't get anything round here.'

'See, if you thought Amos really wanted the plot, I'd drop a word in my pal's ear. Thought it'd give Amos something to think about instead o' worrying about Dolly.'

'You could be right,' Sam agreed.

'You think he'd really work at it if he got it?'

Sam eyed him. There was a glint in those black eyes. Seth was up to mischief.

'You're not thinking of charging Amos a fee for getting him the plot?'

'Sam! Would I do a thing like that?'

They looked at each other. Sam didn't need to say, 'Yes,

you would.' After a moment Seth said: 'Thing is, this plot needs a bit of attention. Been neglected, see? Old Mrs Bainwood had it and it got a bit much for her. So it ought to go to somebody who's really going to put their mind to it. Amos likely to do that?'

'You know Amos,' Sam said. 'If he takes it, he'll work at it. He never does anything by halves.'

'Right, I'll tell Howard. Nice, isn't it – to be able to do a good turn for a friend.'

'Hm,' Sam said, and pushed the plate of parkin at him. 'Have another biscuit, Seth, and stop trying to look as if butter wouldn't melt in your mouth.'

Nevertheless, after Seth had gone, it cheered Sam a lot to think of Amos trying to cope with an allotment. A rank amateur! He'd have to come to Sam for advice, which Sam of course would be only too happy to give him. It made a pleasant change from worrying about Dolly.

Matt and Annie sat in the hospital worrying. It seemed a very long time before the nurse came to beckon to Matt. 'You can go in, Mr Skilbeck, but she's still a bit drowsy and very weak. Don't stay long, and don't upset her.'

Matt nodded wordlessly. He went into the quiet ward, next door to the recovery room, where relatives were allowed a quick word with a post-operative patient before she was removed to the main ward.

He was shocked at how different Dolly looked as he reached her side. There seemed no flesh on her bones. Her eyes looked huge in her white face. Her fair hair was pulled back and tied with a piece of white bandage at the nape of her neck; it seemed to have lost colour and lustre.

Although her eyes were open, she didn't look at Matt.

'How're you feeling, love?' he asked scarcely above a whisper.

She let her head roll over so that she met his gaze. She made no reply.

'You'll feel better soon,' he said.

She made a tiny movement of negation. 'No, I won't.'

'The doctor said – '

'I won't feel better. I'll never forgive myself.'

'What?' Matt took the hand lying limply on the coverlet. 'You've nowt to blame yourself for, Dolly – '

'I couldn't even have your baby,' she said in a weak, bitter voice. Then she turned her head away from him, closed her eyes, and let her hand slip out of his grasp in rejection of all comfort.

Chapter Two

When Dolly was taken up to the main ward, she slipped back into sleep. The ward sister told Matt that if he waited he might see her again when she woke. But no other visitors would be allowed today, so she recommended that Annie should go home.

'I'll stay with you outside till she wakes, Matt – '

'Nay, Annie, you go home. They'll be needing their tea soon, and you've your poultry to see to and the geese – '

'Joe or Grandad will do that – '

'Joe's got plenty to do as it is. And Grandad's probably trying to do the cooking.' Matt summoned a smile. 'You wouldn't inflict that on Joe, would you?'

'They'll manage – '

'You go on home,' he said. 'I'll be poor company anyhow.'

'I was thinking of being company for *you* – '

He gave a half shake of the head. 'I'd sooner be on my own,' he said. And then, realizing how hurtful that might sound, he added quickly, 'I don't feel like . . . talking or . . . you know . . . being bothered.'

'Right.' She pressed his hand in a gesture of understanding. 'You'll ring when you've seen her again?'

'Aye, I'll let you know how she is.'

Still uncertain she was doing the right thing, Annie agreed to go, taking her own car and reminding Matt to let them know when he was coming home so they could come to fetch him.

She found her father sitting at the kitchen table peeling

potatoes. He put the task aside with relief when she came in. 'Ah, lass,' he said, 'I'm glad to see thee! What's the news?'

'Matt saw her, they wouldn't let me. He's waiting until she wakes up again and then he'll ring us.'

'What do they say about her?'

She shook her head. 'The operation was a success, if you can call it that. But she's very weak and still has a high temperature. I think she'll need careful nursing, poor lass.'

He questioned her until he'd got every detail she could remember. Then, seeing her sad expression as she tied on her apron, he suddenly bethought himself of good news. 'Hey-up, what d'you think? Jack rang from Rome. He's coming home!'

'What?' She turned so suddenly that the bowl of potatoes in water slopped over in a tide of grey on to her spotless table. She didn't even notice. 'Coming home?'

'Aye, he talked to Joe. Couldn't quite get the hang of it but he said he'd try to ring again to let you have a firm date.'

'Good heavens, you mean you didn't find out what day he's coming?'

'Didn't seem to know. Sitha, lass, you know what our Jack's like. If you ask me, the idea had just occurred to him that morning and he hadn't looked up air schedules or owt like that.'

'How long is he coming for?'

'Didn't say.' Sam chuckled. 'Comes and goes like t'cuckoo, doesn't he! Any road, he'll tell you all that when he phones again.'

'I must get his room ready,' Annie said, putting down the bowl of potatoes and making for the door to the stairs.

'Hi, Annie, you can do that after you've started tea!'

'I'll just run up and have a look. I meant to take down the curtains in the spare room last week, but I didn't get round to it. I wonder if I could just take them down now and put them in the machine – '

'Annie, Joe and I only had cold meat and pickle for dinner,' Sam groaned. 'Look at the curtains after you get summat on t'stove for tea!'

But there was no doubt he'd achieved his aim – Annie

looked quite different when she went back to peel the potatoes.

She cross-examined Joe when he came in for his food, but learnt very little. After she had cleared the table and washed up, she threw herself into a flurry of activity. When the phone rang, she darted to it, expecting Jack to be on the other end, giving her the time of his plane's touchdown at Manchester Airport. She was almost shocked when she heard Matt's voice. He was telling her he'd seen Dolly, that she was a little better but that he wasn't to see her again this evening.

'I think I might as well come home,' he said. 'They tell me she's out of danger and I can come in again in the morning.'

'I'll fetch him,' Joe pantomimed to his mother.

'Joe's coming to pick you up,' Annie said.

'Nay,' Matt said. 'Tell him not to. I'll go and . . . have a bite to eat somewhere. And then I'll get a bus to Hotten, and . . . and . . . oh, I'll get a lift, or a taxi, or summat.'

She was about to protest that he'd do no such thing, but then she realized he needed to be alone. He had to come to terms with what had happened.

Not for the first time, tragedy had struck Matt Skilbeck. He had lost his first wife, Annie's daughter Peggy, through a totally unexpected illness. Left with two small children to look after, he had in the end let them go to stay with a middle-aged aunt and uncle. His aunt and the twins had been killed in a train crash.

It had been a long time before Matt looked about him to see that the world still had something to offer him. At length he had found Dolly, and now their child had been taken from them before it ever saw the light of day.

He needed to spend some time alone with the realization of the tragedy. He didn't want to talk, to put up a front. Seldom seen to make a fuss, he wanted to grieve in silence out of sight of others.

It was quite late when he at last let himself into the farmhouse, but he already knew by the light gleaming from the window that someone was still up, and he knew it would be Annie.

'You should have gone to bed, Ma,' he protested.

'I couldn't go without knowing you were all right, lad.'

'I'm fine. I had a long walk around Hotten then I had a meal and a pint and a think, and then I got a lift from Mr Anstey.'

'That's not what I meant, Matt.'

He hesitated. 'I'm all right. I see now that I'm lucky to have Dolly still with me, even if we lost the baby. I don't know what I'd have done if I'd lost Dolly, Ma.'

'Let's hope that never happens.'

'I thought about it all, and I realized that we've never really had the baby. Never held it, talked nonsense to it. Poor little mite, it never really existed.'

'Aye, that's true enough.'

'Dolly doesn't see it that way – she's grieving. But I hope she'll . . . get over it.'

'Yes, and she will. She's a sensible lass.'

'So that's the way of it, Ma. Don't you fret about it. We've survived worse than this, you and me.'

'That's right, lad,' she sighed. She got up. 'Shall I make you a hot drink?'

'Nay, I'm for bed. I'm just going to ring and ask the night sister if Dolly's sleeping quietly and then I'll get some sleep myself.'

Next morning she had the spare room curtains out on the line almost at break of day. She got Matt to move a comfortable chair into the spare room so that Jack could sit there to read if he wanted to. She tried to find a suitable table for his typewriter but nothing they owned seemed to be the right height. She stayed near the phone in case he should ring with information about his flight. Though she needed food supplies from the shop, she sent Judy Westrop to fetch them rather than leave the house and miss his phone call.

Had she only known it, she was wasting her concern. Her son Jack was already in Beckindale, walking down the High Street with a portable typewriter in one hand and a suitcase in the other. Nearly two hours had gone by since he landed at Manchester Airport. Typically, he'd taken the airport bus into the city, caught a train to Hotten, and come on the bus to Beckindale. As to letting his mother know, that had never really figured in his plans.

Seth Armstrong, heading for the churchyard to filch some yew twigs, slowed his loping pace at sight of him. 'Hey-up . . . Jack Sugden?'

'Hello, Seth.'

'I didn't know you were coming?'

'Only let Ma know yesterday.'

'Home on holiday?' Seth said, holding out his hand.

Jack set down his suitcase and shook hands. 'More or less. I hear you've gone over to the bosses' side, Seth – turned gamekeeper?'

'Oh aye, dead respectable.' Seth winked. He saw Jack glance about. 'Doesn't change much, does it?'

'No,' Jack said, with a suppressed sigh, 'it doesn't.'

'Want a lift up to t'farm? Judy Westrop's going up there in a minute – she's in t'shop, getting sugar and tea and stuff for your ma.'

'Nay, I'd like to walk,' Jack said. 'See you, Seth.'

'Aye,' said Seth, and watched him walk on.

He saw a tall, upright man in his thirties, dressed in well-made corduroys and a jacket of Italian leather – a bit too smart for Beckindale, thought Seth, but not as dressy as some townies. For Jack was a townie these days, no getting away from it. His skin had the smooth look that came from living under a gentler, sunnier climate than the Dales. Though he was carrying his cases easily, he didn't walk with the force that a countryman could have put into it. His dark, gypsy-black hair was well-barbered, he was even wearing suede shoes. Seth remembered a time when Jack Sugden thought suede shoes were cissy.

'He's a funny one,' Seth thought to himself. 'Keeps coming back – can't seem to stay away despite the pleasures of *la dolce vita*. Bit sad, this homecoming, though – wi' Dolly in hospital.'

Jack continued on his way, well aware that Seth was watching him. 'Thinks I've gone soft,' he mused to himself. 'Well, happen he's right. These bits of luggage seem to weigh a ton. Trees well out, I see – somehow I fancied they'd still be in bud, but after all though this is north of Rome it isn't Siberia. Joe's been working on the field-walls – not a break to be seen. Bye! He's even got gates with catches on them, not bits of string. Sheep look good – that's Matt, of course. Where's the milk herd? Gone up the hill, happen – is there enough grass up there by now?'

He turned into the lane to the house.

Sam was sitting in his chair, working on a small piece of carving. Annie was just sewing the last loose curtain ring on the curtains for Jack's room. The phone rang. 'That'll be him!' she exclaimed, jumping up.

But it was the vicar. 'Nay, I didn't tell you because I heard only yesterday, vicar,' she replied to his surprised enquiry. 'I'm waiting to hear . . .'

A knock came on the door. Sam, grumbling, got up to open it. There was a moment's pause.

'I'll be going to meet him,' Annie said into the phone.

'Then you won't have to go far,' her father remarked.

Annie turned.

'Hello, Ma,' said her son.

'Jack!' She dropped the phone and ran to greet him. It was only some minutes later that Sam, noticing the receiver quacking in enquiry, picked it up and replaced it sharply, feeling a small triumph in silencing it.

'I were going to come and pick you up, Jack,' she cried, hugging him.

'I wanted to walk it, Ma.'

She understood only too well. He needed that interval to acclimatize himself, to see his old world again and understand he still had a place in it.

'Welcome home, lad.'

'Aye,' Sam echoed, 'welcome back.'

'You'll be parched for a cup of tea,' Annie went on. 'Or coffee?'

'It's usually coffee about now, isn't it?'

'Aye, you still remember the routine, do you? And scones – I made scones, remembering how you like them with fresh butter.'

'Where's Joe?'

'He's up at the Home Farm having a chat wi' Richard Anstey – that's the assistant manager up there, there's a bit of trouble over a bullock that got out and caused some damage. He'll be back for elevenses, never fear.' Annie busied herself clearing the newly-ironed curtains off the table so she could put out the mugs and plates, and at the same time brought Jack up to date on all the news.

'How's Matt taking it?' Jack asked. 'I mean – when he comes in – can it be talked about?'

'Oh, aye, he's being very calm. It's Dolly, really – it's a big thing for a woman, to lose a babby,' Annie sighed. 'But by the time she comes home I expect she'll be over the worst.'

'Did you bring my courgette seeds, Jack?' Sam put in.

'Nay, forgot all about it. In any case, I think it's illegal, bringing seeds in without a permit. But I brought you this instead,' he said with a grin, and produced a bottle of Chianti.

'Can't plant that,' his grandfather grumbled.

'But you can sink it.'

They laughed. Annie said, 'We'll have it tonight, eh? I'll do summat special, we'll have a welcome home party.'

'Er . . . Would that be appropriate?' Jack queried. 'In view of Dolly . . . ?'

'We're not going to go mad, Jack. Just a glass of wine and a special dish to let you know your homecoming's a pleasure to us.'

As Annie made the coffee, Jack asked if he could go up and change. 'I feel a bit of a fashion plate in this gear,' he confessed. 'Seemed all right in the Via Veneto, but feels wrong here.'

'Oh, I haven't got your curtains up yet – '

'It's all right, Ma, I promise not to stand in front of t'windows while I change – not that there's anything to see me except rooks in the branches!'

When Joe came in, looking slightly miffed after his interview with Richard Anstey, Jack was coming downstairs in jeans and a sweater. Joe paused in the act of pulling out a chair to sit down.

'Well, I'll pick taters with tongs,' he said. 'It's Big Brother!'

'How's things, Joe?'

'You didn't waste much time! Last words we exchanged, you were in Rome.'

'The wonders of modern travel.'

'You look good, Jack.'

'I'm fine. How're you?'

'Peeved. Anstey is being sticky about the wall that beast pushed through. I don't think I'll pursue it, though – I'd rather stay on good terms with him if I can, even if he is to blame for not keeping his bullocks properly penned up.' Joe glanced about. 'Matt not in yet?'

'He'll be here.'

'Happen not. I think he decided to work through, and get off to the hospital mid-afternoon. Of course,' Joe added, with an ironic glance at his elder brother, 'he wasn't to know the Man from Mars was going to be here at coffee time.'

'Tell you what, I'll take his coffee out to him,' Jack suggested. 'Where is he?'

'Up Grey Top, sorting out ewes for show.' Joe gave a sly grin. 'It's a longish walk. Sure you're up to it, after years of easy living?'

Jack aimed a mock punch at him. 'You be careful, young 'un. I used to cuff your ear and I could easily get into the habit again.'

When coffee was over, Jack accepted a flask of coffee and two buttered scones from Annie to take to Matt. He and Joe went out together.

'Er . . . if you don't mind me asking,' Joe said, 'what's behind all this?'

'All what?'

'This sudden trip home.'

'I don't think it's any more sudden than any other trip I've made.'

'You can say that again! Now you see him, now you don't. But you generally have a reason for coming back. Last time, if I remember rightly, it was to get away from some actress who thought she wanted to marry you.'

Jack Sugden looked at his brother with an expression in which there was something almost like sadness. 'You don't really believe all that rubbish they used to print about me in the papers?'

'I believe it when they say that book of yours was mainly autobiographical – and you have to admit, Jack, it was a bit warm. I think most of us would think a woman was involved in any sudden decision you made.'

'Well, they'd be wrong this time, at any rate,' Jack said, with a glint of anger in his black eyes. 'If you want to know, I've come home for a bit of peace and quiet.'

'As opposed to what? The chink of money in your bank account? The chatter at literary cocktail parties?'

'As opposed to the madhouse that Rome's turned into this last few years. It's a beautiful city, Joe, but strangling to death in a tangle of traffic.' Jack sighed and shook his head. 'When I first went there to live, it was a golden place. Rome seemed to be a sort of dream city, all marble and the dark of cypress trees. But it's a different sort of darkness now, and the marble is cracking under the vibration of the juggernaut lorries. I just suddenly felt . . . it would be nice to take a look at Emmerdale again.'

Joe thought about it, and then decided to ask the question. 'Staying long?'

'That depends.'

'On what?'

'I'm supposed to be writing a book. A travel book, about the Dales. I'll have to see how it goes.'

'Humph,' said Joe. 'Well, you know your way to Grey Top, eh? Matt'll be by the old sheep pens round behind Barkle Crag. See you at dinner time.'

He parted from Jack, making his way to the barn. They'd be making silage soon if this dry weather kept up. He needed to see if there was storage space and ponder on whether or not to extend the barn. He couldn't help remembering what Richard Anstey had just been telling him – that Maurice Westrop, the manager at N.Y. Estates, was considering an offer to go to Wales for the company and, with almost unlimited funds, set up a new milk-producing farm on modern lines. Unlimited funds! What a pleasure it would be never to have to stop and worry about ten pounds, twenty pounds, for necessary equipment. Joe didn't want to handle thousands, he would just have liked not to be always looking at the pennies.

Not for the first time, Joe thought about Jack's money. Jack had made a fortune with his book, which had been a runaway bestseller. Then he'd made another fortune with the film rights, and the film was still being shown from time to time even now: it was one of those that had turned into a modern classic. What had Jack done with it all? Had he thrown it away in riotous living in Rome? If not, would he ever consider investing some of it in the farm? Jack was a partner, but not a very active one. The fact that he'd suddenly come home might mean a renewed interest, however temporary, in the well-being of Emmerdale Farm. Joe would never think of asking outright for an investment from Jack, but if Henry ever thought of mentioning it to him something might come of it.

On his way back from taking Matt his elevenses, Jack took a stroll round the farm. It had been extended since last he was home; he couldn't help being impressed by the well-cared-for fields and the healthy livestock. By the time he had finished his survey, it was opening time at the Woolpack. He decided to drop in and say hello to Amos.

The landlord of the inn was holding forth as Jack entered. 'The fruits of the earth,' he was saying, 'properly cooked, or eaten raw where appropriate . . . That's the kind of diet that keeps choresterol – '

'Cholesterol,' Henry corrected.

'That's what I said, Mr Wilks – choresterol must be kept in check. Fresh vegetables, straight from the soil and washed as little as possible so as not to destroy the vitamins – ' Amos broke off. 'Jack Sugden!'

'How do, Amos. Has the beer improved since I was last here?'

Amos opened his mouth to protest that his beer was good, always had been good, and always would be good. But he understood after a split second that he was being teased, and in any case Henry forestalled him.

'Beer, nothing! Have something more appropriate – on the house, Jack.'

'I'll still have a beer, thanks. You know Grandad says, the Italians don't understand about beer. And he's right an' all. Pint please, Henry.'

'Annie said you were coming,' Henry went on as he pulled the pint for him. 'But I didn't gather you were expected so soon.'

'Seemed no reason to hang about once I'd decided,' Jack said. 'How's business?' He eyed the small gathering of locals, who nodded at him in greeting as they met his glance.

'Always quiet at lunch-time on a Tuesday,' Amos said. 'What's the news on Dolly, Jack?'

'I was just talking to Matt about her. He rang early this morning. Making progress, they said. He's going to see her this afternoon.'

A very attractive girl of about twenty-nine or thirty walked in, with loose soft hair caught back by a fine woollen scarf and a slender figure masked by a short quilted jacket. 'Morning, Judy,' Henry said. 'Usual?'

'Yes, please.' She turned to look at Jack. 'You must be Jack Sugden. I've been dying to meet you.'

Jack was a little taken aback. He was accustomed to women greeting him eagerly, but he didn't quite expect a gushing opening from a girl like this. He discovered in a moment that she meant it literally, however. 'I'm Judy Westrop, a friend of your mother's – I was in the stores doing her shopping for her when you arrived. When I got up to the farm Annie told me I'd just missed you.'

'You mean you tracked me all the way round Emmerdale to the pub?' he laughed.

'No, that's sheer good luck.' She accepted her drink from Henry. Jack was interested to note that it was pure orange juice.

He was intrigued. People always interested him. He fell into chat with her and though he hadn't expected to discuss his forthcoming book, gave her a few details. 'It's what you call a personalized travel book,' he explained. 'Bit of what I know about the north of England decked out with fancy prose.'

She studied him. 'You don't actually seem to think too highly of it?'

My word, she's bright, he said to himself. He hadn't meant to let it show, his opinion of this silly deal his agent had set up for him. A travel book about the Dales – who the devil wanted to know Jack Sugden's opinion of the Dales? He was no historian, no expert on wild life. The book he'd written with the help of his grandfather, about the old life of Beckindale, had sunk like a lead balloon. What reason was there to think that this book would be any different?

Jack was coming to the conclusion that he was a one-book author. It's often said that every human being has one book in him, and it might well be that Jack had written his. He'd done well out of it, and done even better out of the film script – but since then nothing he'd written measured up to his own standards of excellence. It was as if he had nothing else of importance to say. Once before he'd come home in search of inspiration, with his agent hammering at him to get started so as to fulfil the contract he had made for him. The novel he'd been trying to write had died on him. In final desperation, Philip had got the contract altered to admit of a non-fiction book instead of fiction, so now here he was, back home, trying to steel himself to the task of poetizing about the landscape – a landscape he loved but hadn't seer for years. The only way this book was going to be a success was if the publisher sold it as 'by Jack Sugden, author of *Field of Tares*': it had no other value for there were hundreds of men who knew more about the architecture and customs of the Dales than Jack Sugden. And Jack knew very well how the reviewers would treat it. 'Relying on his name as a best-selling author of sexually explicit novels – valueless as a contribution to travel writing . . .'

Amos approached, anxious to get a few details for inclusion in his piece for the *Hotten Courier*. 'Local Author Returns Home: Jack Sugden of Emmerdale Visits Birthplace.' Could you use the term 'birthplace' in connection with a famous person still living? Or did that only apply to dead geniuses? Perhaps it would be better to use the word 'roots'. Fashionable, that was, after that TV series. Jack Sugden returns to his Roots – not bad, that. And speaking of roots . . .

'What's happening about my application for an allotment, Seth?' Amos asked, moving along the bar to the gamekeeper, who had been there for five minutes or so with his nose buried in a pint pot.

'Aye, well, when you've finished hobnobbing with the famous, lad,' Seth grumbled, 'I've got a bit o' news for thee. I had a word with that pal o' mine on the committee – and the long and short o' it is, they've got a plot.'

'Got a plot?' Amos reared back like a nervy horse. It sounded ominous.

'Of land, I mean,' Seth said. 'Bit of luck, isn't it? If you get cracking on it now, you'll have summat ready to put in t'Show.'

'The Show?'

'Flower Show.'

'I'm not going to waste my land on flowers, Seth,' Amos said with hauteur. 'I'm going in for vegetables to help win the battle against tinned and frozen food.'

'Good for thee,' Seth said. His black eyes glinted with appreciation. 'But you know as well as I do, since you do reports on it for t'*Courier*, that the Show's got veg in it as well as flowers.'

'Oh . . . of course . . .'

'You might try pitting yourself against me and Sam for our pot leeks,' Seth said. 'Or green peas – six of a variety, free of all blemish or insect marks, uniform in length and each with the same number of peas in the pod . . .'

'Green peas,' murmured Amos, picturing his peas climbing up their green nylon netting on his plot.

'Or beans. Beans are easy to grow – '

'I'm not after what's easy,' Amos interrupted in indignation. 'Adding variety and interest to the diet, that's the intention – us folk that's come to understand about wholefood know that to compensate for the loss of convenience foods like fish fingers, we have to add variety to the meal. Courgettes, broccoli – '

'You're going to grow broccoli?' Seth said. 'That should be interesting.'

'I'll do some research on it. That's what a journalist does, sitha – he looks up background information and gets to know the ins and outs afore he plunges in. I'll just do a bit of reading-up on it and see if broccoli's a good crop to go in for.'

'Aye,' said Seth. 'Buy a book, that's what I'd do if I were you, Amos. Should be interesting.'

'Well . . . thanks, Seth, for helping me get the allotment,' Amos said in awkward appreciation. 'Er . . . have one on me, eh? Your usual?'

'Since this is a special occasion I'll have – '

'A pint of old?' Amos interrupted with haste. He knew Seth too well to let him name his poison. Double whisky, it would have been. He drew the beer and gave it to him. Seth, with a sharp glance at him, buried his face in the tankard as if to hide a grin.

Maurice Westrop, the manager of N.Y. Estates, came into the bar rather hurriedly. 'Oh, there you are, love,' he said on seeing his daughter.

Jack couldn't help observing he looked with anxiety at Judy's glass. She held it out to him with a grin. 'My usual,' she said, mischief in her voice.

'Oh . . . ah . . . I was just going to say – I'm on my way home for lunch, if you want a lift.'

'Thanks, I was just thinking of making a move.' She swallowed the small amount of orange juice remaining in her glass. 'Nice to have met you, Jack,' she said as she got up. 'I hope we'll have a chance to talk some more about your views on writing. I'm helping Annie while Dolly's poorly so I'll see you around, huh?'

'Hope so,' Jack said, and watched her go, thinking to himself that there was a girl with problems.

But who hadn't? He himself was no exception. And he'd have to come to some decision fairly soon. He couldn't go on pussyfooting like this.

Judy got into the car with her father. He glanced at her with a smile. 'That was Jack Sugden, then?'

'Yes, he seems very nice – interesting.'

'More interesting than Joe?' he teased.

'Different. Mind you, though it's fascinating to hear about the people he met through his book, I can't see that it has much relevance to life here in Beckindale.'

'Well, he's not likely to stop. I gather he's been here before and gone away again.'

'Yes. He hasn't learnt yet that roving around doesn't do you too much good.'

Maurice concentrated on taking the turn round Sloper's Lane to the Home Farm. 'Are you saying you've learnt it?'

'Well, Father, you have to admit I've moved about the country with you since Mother died, and haven't found it too rewarding.'

'Well now . . . that brings me to something I have to talk to you about.'

'Wales?'

He nodded, drove into the forecourt of Home Farm, and drew up. 'Let's get lunch on the table and then we can talk,' he suggested.

They went indoors. While Maurice opened a tin of soup and heated it up, Judy made sandwiches of cold meat and salad. They sat down at the modern kitchen table to eat. The May sunlight poured in; there was warmth and richness in the golden rays. June was just around the corner, with all its summer wealth. And if Maurice Westrop was going to Abergrug to start the new milking herd, he ought to go soon, to break the back of preparations before the autumn.

'Are you thinking of taking the job in Wales?' Judy began, spooning up her first taste of soup and nodding in appreciation.

'It's like this, my dear. It's a good post, a step up – and after all I'm fifty-two, I'm not going to get many more of those. So of course I'm drawn to it. But . . .'

'What?'

'Only if you want to go.'

'Me?' She looked up, setting the spoon down and staring at him. 'Why does that matter so much?'

'Well . . . surely, love . . . you can see I wouldn't go without you.'

She held his eyes for a moment, then drooped her head. 'You mean you feel you can't trust me if you leave me on my own?'

'Of course I didn't mean that!' But there was too much vehemence in his tone.

'It's all right, Daddy. I'm over all that. I understand now that I have an extreme sensitivity to alcohol and that I must avoid it. I don't feel the need of it any more. You can trust me to stay on an even keel if we go our separate ways.'

'But . . . Would you want to do that? Is that what you're telling me?'

'The decision is yours, really, isn't it? You're the one who wants to move on. Until I went to make my own life in the woollen towns, I just went along with your decisions – I moved from place to place, from estate to estate – it merely meant a different roof over our heads because I'd no friends worth mentioning. We hardly seemed to stay long enough anywhere for me to make any.'

'Judy!'

'I'm not blaming you. I suppose I got wary about making friendships, even at school, because I suspected they weren't going to last long. I remember one girl at St Margaret's College – we swore to write to each other every week.' She smiled and sighed. 'It lasted a fortnight. Two letters from me to her, two from her to me. We'd really nothing in common after that. But it's different now, Father. I feel I've a lot in common with the people here.'

'In Beckindale?' Maurice said in surprise. 'What's so different about Beckindale?' And then, pressing his lips together, 'Joe Sugden?'

'He's part of it. We're friends. But it's more than that. When I came out of the clinic, feeling sort of vulnerable and scared at facing the world again, Beckindale welcomed me. People cared – the vicar, Annie Sugden, Dolly Skilbeck . . . It felt like coming home when I looked out of the car and saw the church and the village green. I don't want to leave it and start again, you see. Not yet, at any rate.'

'That's that then,' Maurice said. 'I'll let N.Y. Estates know that I don't want the job.'

'No, don't do that, Father!'

'But I can't move on and leave you, my dear. We've really only just . . . begun to know each other. I don't want to throw that away – '

'You won't be throwing it away. We've learnt a lot. If I'd carried on with my job in the ordinary way, I'd be in town now and you'd be on your own here. We'd be keeping in touch, we'd be close despite the separation.'

'Oh, Judy, I hate to think of you trying to cope on your own – '

'But I shan't be on my own, shall I? I'll have my friends. You're the one I'm sorry for – off to start all over again, like a hundred times before, with new people in a new place.' She held out her hand to him suddenly. 'Perhaps I ought to go with you! It's not fair on *you* – '

'Oh, I'm used to it. Don't worry about me. I was just feeling that . . . we might drift away from each other.'

'That's not likely now, Daddy. We've learnt to talk to each other. It's taken us long enough, heaven knows! We're not likely to forget how when it's been so painful to learn it.'

'I know what you mean about friends here,' Maurice said, pressing her fingers in his. 'But all the same . . . I wish you'd come with me.'

'I'll think about it. But the answer will probably be no.'

'You really want to stay on here on your own? I mean, where will you live?'

'I'll find somewhere.'

'But what will you do? Granted your recuperation is still going on, but by and by you'll want a job – '

'Not much demand for a textile engineer in Beckindale, you mean? I'll find something, don't worry.'

He sighed, started to say something, stopped, then decided to go on with it. 'You're not putting too much importance on Joe?'

She shook her head.

'Because . . . I don't mean to interfere but . . . Joe's had his troubles in the past. He isn't going to rush into any relationship with a woman. What I'm trying to say is, don't get too dependent on him.'

'I'll bear that in mind, Daddy.'

She got up to fetch the sandwiches. He watched her moving about in the kitchen. Despite what she said about her feelings for Joe, he was desperately worried.

He liked Joe. A sensible, capable farmer, a good-hearted fellow, from a family respected and liked throughout the Dales. Good son-in-law material, you might say. If Maurice Westrop had thought Joe might ask Judy to marry him, he'd have been only too happy.

But he sensed Joe was steering clear of close personal relationships for the present – and for a reason Maurice well understood. He himself had felt the thing that was now stirring in Joe Sugden.

That new impulse was . . . ambition.

Chapter Three

The news on Dolly's phsyical condition continued to be good. She was allowed visitors. After a few days even Jack went into Bradford to see her, and came away dubious about her reactions to what had happened.

When he got home he found a stranger sitting with Matt and Joe, having afternoon tea. 'You haven't met Geoff Atwill, have you, Jack?'

'Oh, the museum man? How d'you do! I've heard a lot about you from Grandad.'

'Aye, Sam's been a tower of strength to me, identifying horse furniture and so forth,' Atwill said, nodding with satisfaction. 'I came to ask him to cast his eye over these pictures – I'm thinking of bidding for them at Huxley's next week and I wanted to ask his opinion.'

'Where is Grandad, by the way?'

'Out with Seth on some ploy,' Matt said. 'I dunno what

they're up to, those two. Grinning like Cheshire cats, they were.'

'It'll only end in tears,' Joe quoted, nodding his head sagely. It was a thing his mother used to say to him and Jack when they were planning some mischief.

Matt took the colour pictures Geoff produced. 'Why, that's a Derby wagon.'

'You're an authority, then, Matt?'

'Oh, I wouldn't say authority . . .'

'Get on, don't be modest,' Joe said. 'He knows as much about wagons as I do about making tea, Geoff. And you must admit that after all my care, that's the best cup of tea you've had in many a long day.'

'Do you think I should bid for it?'

'Depends if you want to build up a collection of north country vehicles – '

'Well, that was rather the intention of the museum – '

'Thought it were to show a real old farm in action?' Matt objected. 'Most farmers didn't have more'n one wagon, if they even had that much. Can't say I heard of many farms where they had a collection.'

'Touché,' said Geoff, with a glance of defeat at Jack. 'You see, it's easy to get carried away by enthusiasm . . . And speaking of that, have you heard from Ed Hathersage recently?'

'Never stops writing and telephoning,' Joe replied.

'I wish he'd go a bit careful . . . From what he writes me, he seems to be putting every cent he owns in this new farm of his. And you know, Joe . . . he doesn't really know all that much about the land.'

'True enough. He seriously thought he could make a living for himself and his family on that old Hathersage place.'

'Why don't you talk to him, Joe? Warn him to pull in his horns?'

'I've done what I can. Trouble is, he talks in terms I don't really understand. If I could see fields the size he describes, I might have more idea . . .'

'You couldn't accept his idea and go out there for a stay?'

'Chance would be a fine thing,' Joe said. 'Too much to do here.'
'Busy at the moment?'
'Always busy – but yes, we're just starting on silage.'
'Mm, that is a busy time. You're not spraying at present, are you?'
'No, finished. Why?'
'I saw some very peculiar looking wild flowers on my way here today. In the hedge by Vokins Vale. Dog violets all contorted – thought happen you'd been using a hormone spray?'
'Nope, not us,' Joe said with authority. 'Don't use it – too expensive.'
'I should hope you don't use it!' Jack put in with some heat. 'That stuff is a menace – poisonous sprays should be forbidden by law.'
Joe picked up his teacup and drank before replying. 'If you can tell me a way, big brother, of getting rid of thistles without spraying, I'll use it.'
'They can be cut by hand – that's what we always used to do – '
'Right, tomorrow morning, first thing – out! With a billhook and a pair of stout gloves. We'll find you plenty of thistles to cut, won't we, Matt?'
'It's not practical, Jack,' Matt put in in his quieter tones. 'We have livestock to feed – we can't use a slow method like cutting or uprooting when we need the land to grow food.'
'The trouble with that stuff,' Geoff said, 'is that it can't entirely be kept within the bounds of one field.'
'True enough. A few dog violets may be destroyed. But so long as the damage goes no further than that, I don't think we need to be too worried. One thing we've got plenty of, is dog violets.'
'We won't have if spray is used indiscriminately – '
'But nobody uses it indiscriminately, Jack. We've all learned our lesson.'
'Hm,' said Jack, looking unconvinced.
After Geoff had taken his leave, Matt asked Jack how he'd

found Dolly. 'Looking pretty well, I thought. But she doesn't seem to want to talk much.'

'The doctor says that's to be expected. Ma stayed on when you left, did she?'

'Aye, but I don't think Dolly wanted to chat to her, even.'

'They were saying as they'd need her bed soon. Said they thought it might be a good thing to let her go on to a clinic for a week or two – get really fit.'

'Oh, yes?' Jack said. Joe, catching something in his tone, looked a question, but Jack shook his head ever so slightly.

'Time to be out in the mistle,' Matt said, getting up. 'Thanks for going to visit Dolly, Jack.'

When the door had closed behind him, Joe looked at Jack. 'What was that about?'

'I should imagine the place they want Dolly to go to is a unit for psychotherapy.'

'You what? What on earth is that?'

'A place where you can get help with emotional or . . . mental problems.'

'Mental? You're not saying Dolly's going out of her head?'

'No, but she's suffering from depression, I should think.'

The phone rang, breaking into his explanation. Joe said in annoyance, 'That thing never stops. I'm beginning to think Grandad's right about it.' When he had answered it, he held out the receiver. 'For you.'

Jack accepted it. He heard his literary agent's voice. 'Hello, Jack, is that you? Philip here. Listen, old boy, how's the book coming?'

'It's not.'

'How d'you mean, not? You said that once you got home and slipped back into the feeling of the Dales, you'd be able to write it.'

'Well, I was wrong.'

'Look here, Jack old fellow, you mustn't be negative about it. You must plunge in. You'll find it'll come once you get started.'

'No it won't,' Jack replied. 'I've tried.'

Philip Bardoe was going on at him through the receiver:

deadlines, contractual obligations, publishing schedules. 'I can't, Phil.'

'It's no good saying that, Jack. You *must*.'

'That's easy to say. I can't. It's not that I don't want to. I can't.'

'Look here, Jack, you'd better come down to London and talk this through. I can perhaps get the deadline put off another three months, but you must understand this is the last postponement. Bring your outline of the book and we'll re-plan the timing.'

'What's the point, Phil?'

'What's the point of just letting things go to pot, old chap? We've got to take steps to get the show on the road. What time can you get here?'

'I don't know that I want to – '

'What time – sherry before lunch? Noon-ish?'

'Oh, all right. Where?'

'The Garrick, old boy. And we'll sort it out once and for all. See you.'

Joe had been changing into boots and coat for the milking parlour during this conversation. Jack said, 'I'm going to London tomorrow.'

'What, no thistle-cutting?'

'No, and I shan't be able to help Matt groom his show sheep. Tell him, will you. I'm sorry – it's business.'

Typical, Joe thought as he made his way to join Matt. Right typical, that was. Pretending to get interested in the livestock, but dropping it the minute any of his fancy friends in London crooked a finger. One thing you could rely on with Jack – you couldn't rely on him!

Sam was crossing the yard as Joe went out. 'Hello, Grandad, there's still some tea in the pot if you want it.'

'Nay, lad, I had tea with Seth and his missus.'

'Oh? Been spending the afternoon there?'

'No.' Sam smothered a grin. 'No, we took Amos to introduce him to his new allotment.'

'Oh? Was he pleased?'

'Impressed,' Sam said. 'I think you could definitely say he was impressed.'

The truth was, Amos had been appalled. Sam and Seth Armstrong had gone to the Woolpack at lunch-time to present Amos with the plan of the ground and the letter certifying his tenancy of Plot 21A. They had then betaken themselves to the shed on Seth's plot, to watch Amos find and take possession of the tract.

True to form, he had arrived with the sketch-map, cord and tape measure, and even a stick with a placard bearing his name in Dymo tape, so no one should be under any misapprehension who was the gardener at this plot.

Amos had first headed straight for a tidy-looking little stretch of ground bearing no visible crop and appearing somewhat bare. He consulted his plan, and had just decided that this was not his domain when the owner of the allotment appeared. ''Ere!' he said in annoyance. 'What you doing, prancing round my seedbed?'

'Sorry, sorry,' Amos said. He eyed the other man. 'Mr Connor, isn't it?'

'You know fine and well it is, and if you think you're going to ferret out anything about my method of growing beetroots for the Show, you're on a loser. So clear off!'

'Oh,' said Amos. 'Er . . . sorry. I . . . er . . . was looking for my own piece of land.'

'You what?'

'My plot. I've just got an allotment.'

'Oh, you have, have you? Well, it'll be Mrs Bainwood's piece, won't it – nobody else given up that I know of.'

'Which . . . er . . . was Mrs Bainwood's?' Amos enquired, looking hopefully at a tract adjoining, set out with small seedlings in neat rows.

'Yonder,' said Mr Connor, pointing.

'Oh? Which? The one with the rose bush?'

'Nope – the one where the cow parsley is waving at you.'

'Er . . . cow parsley?'

'That tall stuff – waiting to come out in a white umbrella of flowers.'

This poetic flight of fancy pleased Amos. 'Cow parsley,' he mused. 'That's the common name for summat fine, I s'pose?'

'It's the common name for cow parsley,' growled Mr

Connor. 'Most pernicious weed in Yorkshire – if you except nettles, thistles, creeping buttercup, brambles, ground elder and dandelions.'

Amos gulped, turned in a daze towards his plot, and walked away clutching the sketch-map. Inside Seth's shed, Sam and Seth were convulsed with silent laughter.

Amos trudged up the narrow paths between the allotments until he came to the one where, as Mr Connor had so charmingly put it, the cow parsley was waving.

Old Mrs Bainwood had been falling victim to arthritis for eighteen months now. Once a keen gardener, she had found her work on the plot just too much to go on with, but had felt she'd recover quite soon – or at least one day – and so had not wished to give up the tenancy. Her doctor had at last spoken sharply to her; no more kneeling and twisting after weeds, no more hours spent two-double planting and hoeing. So for about a year nothing had been done to the plot.

So its crop consisted of old bolted spinach and cabbage, bare stalks of brussels sprouts picked by other allotment holders, two or three seed boxes coming to pieces under the ravages of weather, a rake with a broken handle, an old wellington, and a sack containing something which had long mouldered into green moss.

Amos looked at the patch. He looked at the sketch-map. He looked again at the patch. He took out of his pocket his tape measure, the cord with which he had intended to mark out the boundaries of his terrain, his name plate.

Then he said: 'Oh heck!', folded all the items into the plan of the grounds, and threw them down in despair at his feet.

Richard Anstey, taking the shortcut through the allotments to look at the progress of experimental oilseed-rape on a small field beyond, saw the gesture. He shook his head to himself. The landlord of the Woolpack – surely he couldn't be thinking of going in for gardening? You'd think he had enough on his plate as it was, running the inn and acting as stringer for the *Courier*. But there you are, he thought. Dashing off in all directions – that's the trouble with most of the people in this world.

That was one thing you couldn't say about Richard Anstey. Single-minded and clever, he knew just where he was going. He had come to act as assistant to Maurice Westrop only after, with his ear to the ground, he'd heard rumours that Westrop would be moving on soon. Anstey was keen to be given control of a new and expanding acquisition of N.Y. Estates. He wanted to show what he could do.

He was pretty sure Westrop had decided to take the job in Wales. At least, if Anstey were in Westrop's shoes, he'd take it – grab it, almost. But then Westrop seemed to have reservations to do with his daughter.

Anstey had little time for Judy Westrop. There had been some trouble, he gathered – she'd been ill.

Business before pleasure, that was Anstey's view. He was a handsome, tall, quiet man in his mid-thirties, quite unaware that he caused a flutter in the hearts of the local girls. He had no time for that kind of thing. It wasn't that he was cold-blooded – quite the reverse, he could get as heated as anyone else when occasion demanded – but he had come to Beckindale to further his career, not look for romance.

The oilseed-rape was just coming into acid-yellow bud. Rather meagre-looking. It was worth having done it for the evidence, but he and Westrop had already talked it over and decided that the district wasn't really suitable for this valuable crop. It did well in Cambridgeshire, which was Anstey's last locality, but it wasn't going to be worth keeping on with it here.

Back at the Home Farm he found Joe Sugden waiting to discuss who was to rebuild the wall knocked down by the rebellious bullock. For the sake of a quick settlement, Anstey agreed it should be done by his work force. 'I'll have to check that with Mr Westrop, of course, but I'm sure he'll agree.'

'Well, thanks, I'm glad to get shot of that,' Joe said. 'We don't have the number of staff you have, you see, Anstey.'

'Of course, I realize that. And Skilbeck's away a lot at the moment – how is his wife, by the way?'

'Improving, we hear.'

'That's good. And you've got your brother as a stand-in for him, I suppose.'

'Much good he is,' muttered Joe.

'Oh? I understood he was brought up on the farm, just like you?'

'That's right, but it's nigh on ten years now since he first left home and he hasn't done much by way of farming since then. And methods change a lot these days, don't they?'

'That's true.' Anstey rather liked Joe. He sensed an interest in ongoing improvements in farming methods. 'This country is the best in Europe when it comes to keeping up with new ideas,' he said, 'unless you take Denmark, but Denmark is such a special case, having such a limited crop. But one thing's certain – if you want to see farming being treated like a big-scale business, you have to go to the States.'

'Nothing I'd like better,' Joe sighed. 'I've even got an invitation to go. Can't take it, though.'

'Perhaps in a month or two, when Skilbeck's wife is better and he's able to take some of your work?'

'It'll be harvest then. Even our little patch needs two men at harvest time, not counting volunteer helpers.'

'Yes, true enough. It's a pity, Joe. I'd rather have liked to hear what you thought of US farming. We could have compared notes.'

'No chance of that, I'm afraid,' Joe said. He nodded farewell and went out, thinking with some irritation that tomorrow his brother Jack could go swanning off to London for the day, without asking anyone a by-your-leave, whereas he, who wanted to go abroad on a really serious business trip, simply couldn't get the freedom.

He was rather short with Jack later when they met in the Woolpack. Jack seemed not to notice it. He was busy with his own thoughts. He was already looking ahead to his interview with Philip Bardoe, his agent. It wasn't going to be much fun.

He reached the Garrick Club a little after noon next day. The porter directed him to the hall, where Bardoe was waiting for him in a leather armchair. From the wall, portraits of famous actors glared down at them. The Garrick was famous for its association with the arts, hence Bardoe's membership.

During the pre-lunch drink and the meal itself they made small talk. Philip felt it uncivilized to talk business while good food was being served. Afterwards they strolled through the handsome restored piazza of Covent Garden, to Philip's office in Great Russell Street. The office was small, elegant, uncluttered. Philip was looked after by a personal assistant who made sure his surroundings matched his finicky personality.

'Well now, dear man,' he said as he gestured Jack to a chair, 'let's see how far you've got.' He'd already noticed that Jack was carrying no briefcase or folder, and his heart had sunk at the knowledge that, if Jack had done any work at all, it must be possible to fold the pages and put them in a pocket.

'I haven't anything to show you,' Jack said.

'Nothing? But my pet, you said that if you got away from Rome and back to your old homeland, the frozen spring of words would flow . . .'

'I'm sure I never said any such thing.'

'Well, that was the gist of it. Look here, Jack, what have you actually done since you got home?'

'Nothing.'

'Not a single word?'

'Oh, I've put words down, but I've torn them up. I haven't written a single usable paragraph. The fact is, Phil, I not only don't know enough about the Dales – '

'Dear lad, research, research! We can get all that done for you by a paid researcher if you don't want to do it yourself. What kind of birds dwell in the woods, what kind of fish in the streams – '

'You didn't let me finish, Phil. I was going on to say, and what I do know – and that includes the basic facts about birds and fish, let me add – I simply don't want to communicate to anybody else.'

'Don't be silly, J.' Philip was displeased. 'Communication is your business.'

'Is it?'

'Words are a form of communication, Jack. And words are what earn you your bread and butter.'

Jack crossed his feet and regarded the carpet. 'I haven't earned any bread for a long time, Phil. I've been living off the butter of my bestseller.'

'Oh, very witty. But not precisely true. You did a good film script – '

'Only because it was my book and I didn't want somebody else making a mess of it. I didn't do it for the money, you know.'

His agent gave a small shrug. 'Altruism sometimes pays off. I don't complain about that. But if you want to continue in the writing game, Jack, you've got to be more realistic.'

'You've just said the magic words,' said Jack.

'Be realistic?'

'Do I want to continue in the writing game?'

'Pardon?' Philip said, betrayed into inelegance by the question.

'That's what I've come to tell you, boy. I'd have told you before you bought me that expensive lunch if your good manners hadn't forbidden you to discuss business. I've given the matter a lot of thought and I've decided that I don't want to write this travel book.'

'Now look here – '

'I've decided,' Jack said. His tone was unemphatic, but Bardoe knew it was final. 'I should never have let you talk me into it. It was only a better-than-nothing to the problem of my next novel, after all. I couldn't write my second novel, so you fixed up this deal for a travel book. Now I find I can't write this travel book. I can't write it because I don't want to. I don't want to describe to other people what the Dales mean to me. I don't even *know* what the Dales mean to me. I left there in a heck of a hurry when I was a lad, and whether I love the place or hate it, I'm not quite sure. All I know is, I don't think I ought to be writing come-hither prose about it. No doubt there's a good travel book to be written about the Dales but I'm not the man to do it. So I want you to break my contract with the publisher – '

'Jack!'

'I know, it'll cost us money. It can't be helped. Buy the contract out.'

'Good Lord, you'll be lucky if they don't take you to court, messing up their schedules like this at the last minute – '

'They won't do that, old love. It'd be bad publicity, pursuing a poor author suffering from writer's block.'

'If it's just that, Jack – I can arrange another postponement. I mean, they won't be pleased, but if I explain it's that or no book at all – '

'There's no either-or. It's no book at all. I want out.'

'But, dear old J! You can't *do* this – '

'I can. I am.'

'But what the dickens are you going to do with yourself if you don't write?'

'What have I been doing with myself these past four years, since *Field of Tares*? I'll potter around, I'll ponder and wonder . . . and happen in the end I'll know what the purpose is of my presence on this earth.'

'Oh, look here,' Phil said in genuine anxiety. 'A touch of world-weariness is okay in a bestselling author but I don't think you ought to get serious about it – '

'I am serious, Philip. I've reached the stage where I want to know what on earth I'm here for. I thought for a time it was to be a writer, but that seems to have been a blind alley.'

'It's just a phase you're going through,' his agent said, sounding like an anxious mother.

'You might be right. But one thing I've learned – it's a long phase, and living among those trendies in Rome was no way to get through it. At least in Beckindale, the life is real. Getting up at five-thirty in the morning to help with milking is real.'

'Five-thirty?' shuddered Philip, in the tone of one who has never really believed such things existed.

'You see? You and I are from different worlds. I'm going back to the one I came from.'

'But . . . permanently? You can't mean to stay in Beckindale for the rest of your life, J! You'll regret this!'

'I may very well do,' Jack agreed. 'I can't tell you how

much I've regretted other things in my life. But I've decided this is the next step in my journey and I've taken it. So tell the publisher there will be no book from me about the joys of the northern landscape, nor any other book. It's finished, Phil.'

Philip Bardoe didn't give up easily, but after another half hour's arguing he realized he was totally wasting his time. He had always found Jack Sugden a difficult client, apt to go off at half-cock about something that didn't seem in the least important to a businessman like himself. In a way, though it was a pity to lose a talent like his, Philip Bardoe couldn't help feeling a sense of relief. He had struggled for years now to make something of Jack's career. Perhaps after all his failure had nothing to do with a lack of ability on the agent's part – perhaps Jack Sugden simply didn't have what it takes.

They parted amicably enough. Philip promised to get the contract for the travel book ended, at the lowest cost to Jack that he could manage. He would tie up other loose ends, send an accounting in a week or two, and reminded him that there would be small sums of money coming from time to time from the film company and perhaps from renewed paper-back sales of the novel. Try though he might, Jack couldn't rid himself of some of the trappings of the bestseller. And though he might have opted for the simple life, Philip Bardoe had a shrewd suspicion that the money would always come in handy.

Jack left with the feeling that a great burden had been lifted from his shoulders. He was free! He didn't have to sit at his typewriter any more, staring at blank paper in growing despair over his lack of ability.

He walked with a swinging, almost jaunty step back through Covent Garden en route to the nearest coffee house, where he could sit and think over what he had just done. The sun was shining, the air was warm. At a table set out in the market, he ordered black coffee.

He was quite unaware that at a table on the outskirts of the café's lay-out, another man had taken a seat. He had opened a newspaper and was ostensibly reading it. But from time to time he glanced round it at Jack.

Jack Sugden! To Paul Hilleley, it was a godsend. He'd been sent out by his paper, the *Sunday Gazette*, to do a report on a witness in a porno trial. But the witness had been spirited away by his lawyer through a back door, so that no one got a word with him. Hilleley's editor would not have been pleased; the fact that the reporters from the other papers had no better luck wouldn't have mattered.

But as Hilleley came away from the court, cutting through towards Leicester Square, who should he see but Jack Sugden!

So Jack Sugden was in London? Sugden was one of those personalities that newspapers kept track of, one of the jet-set, the café society, from whom they culled their gossip and scandal. He had disappeared from Rome without warning. Rumour had it that there was an angry father threatening a paternity suit on behalf of his daughter, but that kind of thing was always being said about Sugden and half the time nothing came of it.

He ordered a lager and a sandwich, since he'd had no lunch. He watched Jack drink his coffee and order another. By and by Sugden glanced at his watch, and went out of the pedestrian precinct into Henrietta Street. There he captured a taxi putting down its fare, and drove off. Momentarily dashed, Hilleley managed to find another taxi outside Moss Bros and was able to say to the driver, 'Follow that cab!'

To which the driver said laconically, 'Follow it? I'll be alongside it in this traffic.'

It was quite true. The late afternoon traffic was thickening up towards the rush hour. With no trouble at all Hilleley kept Jack's taxi in sight until it set him down at King's Cross. The reporter tumbled out after him and was just in time to see him consulting the departures indicator. Sugden then strolled across the concourse, bought a paper, and made his way on to the platform for the Leeds train. The train was in the station. From the barrier, Hilleley saw Jack step on board.

Wildly Hilleley turned and ran for the nearest phone booth. He got put through to his editor by announcing it was top priority. 'Listen, Pete, I've just found Jack Sugden!'

'Who? Oh, *Field of Tares* – yeah – where?'

'He's on the train for Leeds, Pete – due to leave at ten to five. What d'you want me to do?'

'Get after him, you fool!' cried Chirman. 'Don't lose him!'

'Look, I don't know where this is going to end up – '

'Telephone when you get wherever he's going. I'll see funds are made available. Get going, man, you've only ten minutes to get your ticket!'

'Yes, okay, I'll ring back as soon as I can. 'Bye!'

Luck was with him. Though there was a queue at the ticket office, it moved quickly. He bought a first-class ticket to Leeds, having no idea whether Jack was in a first-class or second-class carriage but having no desire to be turfed out for not having the right ticket once he found him.

He boarded the train with about one minute to spare. He had seen Jack get on about half-way up and found him in a second-class non-smoker. Hilleley made a grimace: too bad, if he'd known he was in a second-class carriage he could have bought a second-class ticket but charged it up in his expenses as first-class. And a non-smoker, too – well, he could always nip out to the smoking part of the carriage if he couldn't hold out against the need for a ciggie.

Jack, quite unaware that he was under surveillance, read his paper and then sat back to watch the countryside unroll outside. There was more pleasure in that now he knew he wasn't going to have to translate it into poetic prose. He saw the fresh green of the trees, the lilac in bloom, some back gardens with roses already out, fields with grain crops at various stages of growth. Let someone else write about it; he was content simply to enjoy it.

He had still to tell his family of his decision. He wasn't quite sure how they would take it. But it couldn't make all that much difference to them. Things would go on just as before except that there would be an extra member to help with the chores. Nothing would disturb the quiet tenor of their ways.

He should have known he was wrong. Life is seldom as quiet as all that, even in a vale in the Yorkshire moors. And the odds were stacked against him, because a reporter from one of Britain's foremost scandal sheets was on his trail.

Not only that but today, during his absence, Pat Merrick and her children had returned to Beckindale.

Chapter Four

The bus had pulled into Beckindale High Street at eleven-forty-five as usual that morning. Amos, coming round the bend from Butter Lane on his bike, faltered and almost fell off at the sight of the young woman standing there with two youngsters at her side as it moved away again. She had a suitcase at her feet, the lad had a holdall, the girl was carrying a basket.

'Hello, Amos – remember me?' the young woman said.

'Course I do.' He didn't quite stammer with surprise, but he could scarcely form the words. 'All right, are you, Pat?'

'Much as usual,' she said. Then with a little nod towards a twitching lace curtain in the cottage along the street, 'And I notice folks still have the usual interest in other folk's business!'

Amos smiled. 'Same the whole world over, I reckon.'

'I suppose so. You haven't seen my two kids in a long while, have you? This is Jackie,' she gave the boy a nudge so that he said ''Lo'. 'This is Sandie – Sandra, really. Say hello to Mr Brearly, Sandie. You've heard me speak of him – Amos, at the Woolpack.'

'Oh, aye.' Sandie gave him a shy grin. 'Pleased to meet you.'

'The pleasure's all mine,' Amos said, and meant it more than a little, for she was a very attractive fourteen-year-old, with long black hair in a square fringe and black, shining eyes. Not that the charms of female persons ever had much effect on Amos.

Yet he'd always thought Patricia Merrick a pretty girl. She still had good looks, although there were fine lines at the edges of her mouth and a few tiny crow's feet at the corners of her brown eyes. She had always been a reticent girl, and now her expression was habitually guarded. Even the smile she now gave Amos had reservation in it.

'On a visit, are you?' he enquired.

'Happen.'

'Staying in the village?'

'Nay, my auntie – you know? Out at Drygrounds – Mrs Harker.'

'Oh, aye – quiet little place. Nice for a holiday.'

But all his fishing wouldn't make her say how long she was staying. By the looks of her luggage, not long. But then it might only mean she'd packed in a hurry, for her husband, Tom Merrick, was the kind of man you might decide to leave when the going got too rough, and then happen you don't hang about deciding which items in your wardrobe to pack.

'Might see you in the Woolpack some evening?' he enquired.

'Might do. Auntie Elsie doesn't approve too much of drinking, though.'

Amos summoned up a recollection of Elsie Harker. Widow, aged about sixty, strict chapel, her house so neat that you could have seen a dropped pin standing out like a broadsword on her carpet. He glanced with hidden sympathy at the two youngsters, casually clad in jeans and faded denim jackets.

Ah well, not his business. 'Nice to see you, then,' he said, and pushed on towards the Woolpack where his partner, Henry Wilks, was coping on his own – inexpertly, as Amos always felt.

'Who was that you were talking to?' Henry enquired as he came in.

'Mr Wilks! You should be looking after the bar, not looking out t'window.'

'Get on with you – there's nobody in but Walter. Who was it?'

'You didn't recognize her?'

'Face seemed a bit familiar, but I can't place her.'

Amos sniffed. It pleased him that these little reminders arose from time to time to show Henry he was still an incomer where he, Amos, was a true pillar of Beckindale.

'You only saw her a few times, I reckon,' he said, then walked away to take his bike round the back.

'Amos!' Henry protested. But he had to wait in patience until his partner reappeared from the back of the inn. Before Amos would continue the conversation he inspected the bar for defects.

Finding none, he deigned to say, 'You don't remember the trouble up at Emmerdale, soon after you came here?'

'Trouble? What kind of trouble?'

'Over *her*.'

Henry cast his mind back. Trouble where girls were concerned suggested Joe, who had had more than one complication in his love life. But the young woman Amos was talking to was surely too old to have been romantically involved with Joe at that time. When Henry first came to Beckindale, Joe was still a lad, and as far as he could recall, the only girl he'd been interested in then was Marian, Henry's daughter.

'Nay, I don't remember,' he confessed.

Amos allowed himself a dignified smile. 'There's some as have good memories and some as haven't. Memory – instant recall – that's what makes a good journalist.'

'So you've remembered who she is – are you going to tell me?'

'Pat Merrick.'

'Merrick . . .'

'Jack's "friend",' Amos said, and sniffed.

Henry hadn't really been aware of the drama acted out all those years ago between Jack Sugden and the Merricks. But there had been enough nods and winks since then, any time Jack was mentioned, to make it clear that he had been considered the village Romeo. People would say they weren't surprised at the things he'd written in that book of his, *Field of Tares* – a right Don Juan, he'd been, you could just imagine him shacking up with different girls once he got to London.

Henry was never sure how much of this was the usual 'wise after the event' attitude. But it certainly seemed clear there had been something between Jack and a local girl – something serious.

A query rose to Henry's mind. He was about to utter it, but checked himself. It was the last thing he ought to say to Amos, who would build it up into some fantasy of fact. Wasn't it odd, though, that Pat Merrick should return to Beckindale so soon after Jack Sugden came home?

Matt came in just before the lunch-time closing, to tell Amos he was off to visit Dolly and would report back on his way home. 'Er . . .' Amos said, and went pink.

'Yes?'

'Hang on a minute, Matt.' He hustled away into the kitchen and reappeared, holding something behind his back. He edged round the bar, came close to Matt, and brought his hand round in a secretive way. 'Er . . . This is for Dolly, with kindest regards,' he muttered. It was a small packet carefully wrapped in pink lettered paper.

'She'll be right pleased, Amos – '

'Ssh,' Amos said, glancing about nervously.

As Matt went out he thought to himself how strange it was that Amos should talk so much about foolish things, yet be so secretive about a kindness.

At the hospital Matt was asked to go first for a chat with a consultant. He was shown into a little office in a wing at the far side of the building. The name plate on the door announced 'Dr Princeman'. He was welcomed in by a plump, middle-aged man with a calm manner.

'Mr Skilbeck? I'm glad you came so early. I wanted to discuss your wife's case with you – '

'Her case?' Matt echoed, alarmed.

'Well, I mean, her condition. Don't be anxious, Mr Skilbeck, there's nothing seriously wrong. But I think you must have realized that she is very depressed.'

'Well, only natural,' Matt said. 'Losing the baby and all . . .'

'You know there is a condition, popularly known as post-natal blues?'

'Oh aye. My first wife . . . She had a day or two of feeling weepy – '

'It's more than that in this case. Partly it's due to a disturbance of the hormone balance and partly to a feeling of guilt – '

'But she's got nothing to be guilty about – !'

'We all have things in our lives we're not very proud of, Mr Skilbeck. In normal circumstances we put them aside, forgive ourselves for our mistakes. But when things go wrong otherwise, we can be haunted by ghosts out of our pasts. Mrs Skilbeck is struggling very hard not to go under, but I think she needs a little help. You've had it mentioned to you, our residential clinic for psychotherapy?'

'You can't mean she's going wrong in the head, doctor – '

'Not at all. It's a simple illness, like 'flu or chicken-pox. It can be treated and cured. But I think Mrs Skilbeck needs just a short period away from the stresses of ordinary life. She's very proud, you know. She wouldn't like anyone to think she was falling short in any way. So she'd struggle too hard to keep a brave face on things, and the strain would be too much for her.'

'I see. That makes sense, I suppose.'

'I want you to persuade her to go to the clinic. She feels it's an admission of defeat, but if you can explain to her that it's simply a way of getting herself fit – like going to a health farm to lose weight, or to the Costa Brava for a suntan . . . ?'

'I dunno . . . If she doesn't want to, I wonder if – '

'But she does want to. She knows she needs to. She just feels you'll think less of her – '

'Oh, for heaven's sake – '

'Exactly, Mr Skilbeck. Can I rely on you, then?'

Matt sighed, then rose and offered his hand. 'I'll talk to her about it,' he said.

Dolly was up, sitting in a cane chair in a sun-room. She looked strange – pale, too composed, and with red rims to her eyes as if she had been crying. Her face lit up momentarily as Matt came in, but she seemed to make a great effort to be casual. 'Hello there,' she said. 'You're an early bird – visiting's just started.'

'You know me,' he said. He kissed her gently. She clung to him for a moment then let go and pushed him towards a chair opposite. He sat down and said, 'How you feeling?'

'Bit shaky physically, but otherwise right as rain. I'm leaving here day after tomorrow.'

'For the clinic?' he asked, plunging in.

'Nay, love, I'm coming home, of course!'

'I've just been having a word wi' that doctor – '

'Oh, him!' she said with an impatient movement of a thin hand, brushing him away. 'Talks rubbish. I'm all right. Temperature's normal, pulse normal – I'm just a bit shaky on my pins but that'll sort itself when I get out and about.'

'Dr Princeman says you ought to go away for a couple of weeks' rest – '

'He's got a nerve!' she said hotly. 'What he means, he wants to put me in a nut-house for two weeks – '

'It's nowt like that, love. He explained it to me. You just need a bit more treatment – '

'Well, I'm not having it! What would Annie say, me going into a place like that?'

'Annie wants what's best for you, love, we all do – '

'Oh, aye, and once it gets round Beckindale that I've had to go to a special clinic they'll all start looking at me sideways when I get back – '

'That's not true, Dolly. They're all concerned for you. I've got messages from everybody, sending good wishes, wanting you to get properly well. Here,' and he fished in his pocket. 'This is from Amos.'

She accepted the packet gingerly, as if it startled her. She read the words all over the wrapping paper – 'get well soon, get well soon' – and a faint smile came to her lips. She untied the inexpert ribbon bow and unfolded the paper. Inside lay a little carton labelled with the name of the cologne Dolly habitually used. A little card was with it: 'I know this is the one you like because you used to use it when you worked for us. Hope to see you back fit and well, Yours faithfully, Amos.'

She sat for a long time looking at the card. Then tears flooded over and ran unchecked down her cheeks. 'Oh, yes,' she whispered, 'I'll go to the clinic and get proper treatment. I owe it to folk who care about me, don't I?'

Matt stayed until the visiting time was up, chatting to her about things in Beckindale: it seemed Maurice Westrop was taking the job in Wales but his daughter would be staying on, Geoff Atwill was having money problems with the farm museum, Joe had had yet another long telephone call from Ed Hathersage urging him to make the trip to the US.

She sometimes listened, but sometimes seemed to drift off into a sad reverie of her own. He left her, anxious yet hopeful that the new treatment at the clinic would make a world of difference. On the way out he sought the psychiatric consultant to report he had got Dolly to agree to go. 'Great!' the doctor said with enthusiasm. 'We'll transfer her tomorrow, then – if you'd like to come about ten-thirty you can go with her and see her settled in.'

'I can go with her?'

'Of course! It's not a prison, you know – just a convalescent home for people with special problems.'

Reassured, Matt went home. En route he called in at the Woolpack. The place was quite busy but Amos spared a moment to speak to Matt. 'How's Dolly, then?'

'Better physically, but a bit pulled down in her feelings, if you see what I mean. She's going to a convalescent place tomorrow, to get herself really fit. She was right pleased with your gift, Amos.'

'Oh, that . . . Huh . . . Well, good health.' Amos put his half of ale in front of him. His glance travelled past Matt to the man sitting at a table by the door. 'Know that feller?' he asked.

'Who? Oh, the skinny dark chap? No, why?'

'Dunno. Something funny about him. I've a trained eye, you know,' Amos said.

'How d'you mean, funny?'

'He's watching everybody.'

'Well, so are you,' Matt remarked.

'Oh, ah – but I'm t'landlord. It's my business to see everybody behaves. Most other folk are more interested in their drink than what's going on around them.'

Matt turned casually to lean his back to the bar and watch the stranger. It was quite true, the man's eyes were everywhere. After a moment his glance met Matt's. He hesitated, gave a half-smile, then came to the bar. 'Same again, innkeeper,' he said, putting his glass on the counter. By the looks of it, he'd just finished a double scotch.

'Nice old pub,' he remarked.

'Kind of you to say so,' Amos replied. He turned to get the refill. Over his shoulder he said, 'Just passing through?'

'No, I fancy I'll stay for a while. You let rooms here?'

'No, we don't, sir, as a matter of fact.' Amos somehow managed to convey that he didn't approve of letting rooms, especially to strangers. He took the fiver the other held out, made change, and waited for the next remark.

'Is there another pub?'

'The Malt Shovel,' Amos said, with a twitch of disdain. 'It's got no accommodation for holidaymakers either.'

'Dear dear. No hotel?'

'The nearest is Connelton,' Matt put in, taking pity on him. 'The Feathers – it's sort of posh but very comfy.'

'Connelton – how far's that?'

'About twenty miles.'

'Mm . . . How do I get there?'

'No car?' Matt asked in surprise.

'Er . . . no . . . I . . .' Inspiration hit Paul Hilleley. 'I've got a Rail Rover ticket – got as far as Hotten with it and then on the spur of the moment took the bus that was standing at the stop. Here I am – Beckindale – nice little place, it looks, but I don't think I can get home tonight, can I? So I better put up at a hotel until the morning.'

'Well, you couldn't do better than the Feathers, I reckon,' Matt said.

'Right, thanks, I'll try there. Can I hire a car to drive there?'

Amos and Matt shook their heads in unison. 'There's a bus at nine-thirty,' Matt volunteered. 'Comes out of Hotten, makes a circular trip back to Hotten, goes via Connelton – takes an hour but that's the only transport unless somebody can give you a lift.'

'Hm . . .' Hilleley sipped his whisky. 'You wouldn't . . . er . . . ? I mean, you seem to know Connelton – if you're going that way I'd appreciate . . .'

'Nay, I live here, at Emmerdale Farm. Sorry. I'd offer you transport but I'm expected back. It's lucky I had summat to eat in Bradford, for even Annie wouldn't be ready to cater for me this hour of the evening.'

'Emmerdale Farm? I suppose it's not a farm where they do bed and breakfast?'

Matt looked regretful. 'Annie would be pleased enough to take you if you were stuck, but with Jack at home, the spare room's occupied.'

'Jack?' repeated the stranger, with an eagerness that surprised Amos.

'Jack Sugden. The Sugdens own Emmerdale Farm.'

'Jack Sugden . . . I seem to know that name?'

'Oh aye,' Amos agreed, looking important. 'He's a bestselling author. Made a name for himself.'

'Of course – *Field of Tares* . . .' Hilleley allowed a knowing expression to cross his face. 'Hot stuff, that was, wasn't it?'

Matt finished his half and pushed himself away from the bar. 'Well, if you'll excuse me, they'll be wondering what's happened to me – I must be off.'

Amos likewise found something to do. 'Excuse me, a customer . . .' he said, and moved away.

Closing ranks, thought Hilleley. So he *lives* here, does he?

After Matt had gone out, the name of Jack Sugden was picked up by one of the locals in the bar. They'd seen him go away and come back on the bus, in his town clothes. Been to Leeds – further, happen. Gone all day. Funny thing, did anybody else notice that Pat Merrick arrived about dinner-time? Oh aye, Pat Merrick. Brought her childer with her. Oh aye, good-looking kids – especially Jackie, eh? Eh? Nudge nudge, wink wink.

Hilleley was fascinated. But he had too much sense to take any part in the conversation. A little after nine-fifteen, Henry Wilks came up to him. 'The bus will be in soon,' he mentioned. 'Thought I'd remind you in case you'd forgotten.'

'Oh, yes, thanks very much. You work here?'
'You could say so – I'm part owner.'
'Oh, 'scuse me. I've enjoyed your pub, Mr – ?'
'Wilks, Henry Wilks.'
'Deserves to be better known. I think I might drop by again in the near future. Does that author, Jack Sugden – does he come in here at all?'
'Certainly he does. You might say this is his local.'
'Is that a fact? I'm interested in him, Mr Wilks. Enjoyed his book. I thought he lived abroad, though?'
'Yes, he does, but he's home for a visit.'
'A long visit?'
Henry gave a chuckle. 'With Jack, there's no way of knowing.'
'But what I mean is, if I came back, say, in a day or two – would he still be here?'
'I imagine so. He's here to write a book about the Dales.'
'I see. Well, ta very much. I'll go out and wait for that bus now. Cheers.' He drank off the last of his whisky and went out.
The drive to Connelton on the bus was long and boring. He booked a room, paying in advance, and ordered a substantial snack in his room. While he waited for it, he rang his editor at his home number in Hampstead. Pete Chirman sparked into anger when he heard his voice. 'Where the devil have you been? The train must have got into Leeds hours ago – I hung on at the office waiting for you to call back!'
'Oh, we went on safari, Pete. I'm in a little place called Connelton, at the back of beyond. Jack Sugden's at his home, Emmerdale Farm, about twenty miles away in a place called Beckindale. I spent a very interesting hour or two at the local inn. Listen, I think we're on to something, Pete!'
'What, for heaven's sake?'
'Well, look here, Jack Sugden's come home ostensibly to write a travel book about the Yorkshire Dales – '
'About what?'
'Yes, can you credit it? As if he'd be bothered! So it's a

cover story, obviously. And what d'you think, squire? An old flame of his just sauntered into town this very day.'

'What old flame? Don't tell me Anita Gridanzi has turned up in the Dales?'

'No, no, this is something quite new! It'll be an exclusive if I can get to the bottom of it. It's a girl called Merrick, Pat Merrick. She seems to be something to do with Sugden's past. But guess what, Pete? She's got a son, just about the right age to have been Sugden's, fathered before he left Beckindale!'

'My, my,' breathed his editor. 'Now that is interesting.'

'I can't fathom why she's come back – whether it's to cause him trouble or whether it's to take up again where they left off. But it'll make a good story, Pete.'

'It certainly will. Look here, you'd better come back first thing in the morning and we'll have a little conference about this. Meanwhile I'll do some research on the place – Beckindale, you said? And see what the morgue can come up with as regards clippings – I've already got out the file on Sugden but there might be something helpful if we look up Beckindale.'

'Okay, Pete. I'll get an early train. I think our quarry's going to stay put here for another day or two, at least.'

He was more right than he knew. For Jack had made an announcement to his family over a cup of coffee provided as refreshment after Matt got back and told his news.

'I saw my agent today,' Jack began. 'I had to talk to him about this book I'm supposed to be writing.'

'How d'you mean, supposed to be?' Joe asked. 'I thought that was what you were doing upstairs?'

'No, I just sat there looking at my typewriter.' Jack smiled with wry amusement. 'Not a rewarding experience. What I wanted to say was, I've chucked it in. I'm not going to write it.'

'Huh!' his grandfather said. 'You're admitting defeat, then?'

'Aye, Grandad, it's a wise man who knows when he's beaten.'

'But you're going to start summat else? Another novel?'

'No,' said Jack. 'I've decided to put away my typewriter.'

There was a silence. Then his mother said, 'What are you going to do, then, lad? It isn't in you to do nothing.'

'I . . . thought I'd work on the farm – if Joe will let me.'

Everyone looked at Joe, who was so taken aback he couldn't speak.

'I used to be pretty handy about the place, Ma,' Jack went on. 'You remember? Dad trained me up to be able to do almost anything.'

'Things've changed, though, Jack,' Sam said, shaking his head. 'Machinery, chemicals, artificial insemination – all new since you used to help your dad.'

'I'm not slow on the uptake, I hope. And though it's a long time since I did a full day's work every day, I've been giving Matt a hand and I don't think he's found me a nuisance?' Jack looked at Matt, who gave an encouraging little nod. 'I don't expect to be paid, Joe. Just let me show what I can do and then make up your mind whether I can come on the strength.'

Joe gave a little frown. 'Thing is, Jack – how long is this idea going to last? I'm not saying you haven't been a help these last few days, and you've certainly made no mistakes – but if you're going to shoot off back to Rome when the notion takes you, I can't say I'm – '

'I won't be going back to Rome. I've given up my flat there.'

'What?' Annie suddenly glowed with pleasure. 'You're thinking of staying permanently?'

'What he means is, he had a bit of a tiff with his agent and told him he was through with writing, then rang long distance to Rome to say he wasn't coming back,' Joe said in a hard tone. 'He could just as easily ring through again tomorrow and say he's changed his mind.'

'No, Joe. I gave up my flat before I ever walked on to the plane for home.'

Everyone looked at him in astonishment.

'It's been in your mind a long time, then,' Matt remarked.

'That's right. It's not sudden. I've been thinking for a long time that I was kidding myself, playing the part of the great writer in his wing of the old palazzo in Rome. It's . . . pretentious, unreal. I got so I was sick of the whole thing. I don't know if you'll understand this, Joe,' he said, turning to his younger brother in appeal. 'You're so used to hard physical work that you're fed up with it, I suppose. But I got to the stage where I felt that the only thing I wanted to do was dig a ditch or chop down a tree. I wanted to be in touch with reality again.'

'It's real enough here, that's certain,' Matt murmured. 'But are you sure you want to get involved on a long-term basis?'

'I'm sure. What I need to know now is, can I stay?'

'Of course you can stay, love,' Annie replied at once. 'This is your home. You've a right to be here.'

'But I've no right to a job here. It's Joe's say-so. How about it, Joe? Will you take me on, on trial?'

Joe hesitated. Sam said: 'Go on, Joe, it's a bargain! You're getting an extra pair of hands for free! And I've been noticing how it's come back to him, the right way of doing things. He's got a way with the animals, you know – always had.'

Joe had few misgivings about Jack's abilities. It was his strength of purpose that worried him. But he felt awkward about continuing the discussion. He shrugged and said he could see nothing against it, but in his heart of hearts he expected his brother to get weary of the whole idea in another month or so.

Everyone was pleased at the idea of Jack settling in permanently. Annie in particular felt as if she had been given a cheque for a million pounds. Jack was her firstborn and, though she would never have admitted it, the nearest to her heart of her children. Peggy she had loved as a mother loves a pretty little daughter, Joe she had loved as the Benjamin of the family, but Jack had been the first child, clever and wayward and affectionate, winding himself around her heart with every one of his tricks and whims. She had been proud of his achievement as a writer and grieved at his absence from home these many years.

Now he was back – for good, so he said. She prayed it might be so.

Matt went out with Joe as Joe set out for his home in Demdyke Row. 'Don't worry about it,' he said. 'He'll be a help, not a hindrance.'

'Oh, I expect he will.'

'What's the matter, then?'

'It just . . . gets my goat a bit, Matt. I suppose I'm jealous, really. He swans away and years go by before he gets in touch. Then he drops in and goes away as he pleases – wouldn't shoulder the responsibility of inheriting the farm, didn't want to know about our problems. All of a sudden here he is, back again, telling us he's always wanted to be in farming.'

'Yes,' Matt said, 'I can see it could be a bit annoying.'

'You think I'm being small-minded? I s'pose I am. But he can do just as he pleases whereas I – '

'Well, you could do as you pleased, Joe, if you wanted to.'

'Oh, could I? Could I? What about this trip to America, then? I'd give my eye teeth to go. But it's no use even thinking about it.'

Matt took Joe's arm. 'Hey,' he said. 'I don't know so much.'

'What?'

'I mean, Joe . . . You can't go to visit Ed because we can't run the farm without at least two men – right?'

'Right . . .' Joe was already beginning to see Matt's point.

'And now, even if you went away, we'd have two men, wouldn't we?'

'But he . . . He doesn't really know enough.'

'I could keep an eye on him.'

'So you could. But do you really think he'll stay?'

'Let's give it a go, Joe,' Matt said. 'See how it turns out.'

'We-ell . . .'

'And if I were you,' Matt added, 'I'd see about a passport and a visa. For if things go all right, you might be heading for the States in a few weeks' time.'

Chapter Five

Paul Hilleley's 'conference' with the editor of the *Sunday Gazette* proved fruitful. The clippings library of the newspaper had come up with some interesting items: some eight years ago there had been a murder in Beckindale, a young girl called Sharon Crossthwaite, and another case more recently in which a poor child had been raped. In the second case the culprit had died in a road accident a few weeks later, right in the centre of the village. But what made the first one more interesting was this: the murderer had served most of his sentence and what with good conduct and so on, he was likely to be released soon.

'What I thought,' Chirman said, leaning back in his chair and pulling a rubber band this way and that, 'was that it'd make a good cover story for you, hanging around the place. I mean, Sugden's no fool. If you start snooping around without any other ostensible motive, he'll catch on. But if you say you're an author planning a book on crimes and their settings, you can stooge around in Beckindale with a good excuse.'

'I use my own car, right? I get mileage expenses on it, as well as subsistence and sums paid out for info?'

'Okay, okay, we've noticed that the only place for you to stay is twenty miles off in Connelton. At least forty miles a day mileage, eh? And more, of course, if you have to dash back and forth several times. Oh, all right, Paul, we'll take everything as kosher, whatever you charge up – so long as you get a story.'

'You're not expecting me to tie Sugden in with these two crimes, are you?' Hilleley said, having flicked through the clippings. 'He wasn't even there when they happened.'

'No, no, nothing like that. No, it's not a crime story we want from you. It's a sex-and-human-conflict piece. What about this girl, Pat What's-it? Is she a looker?'

'Haven't seen her yet. But if you think of the women

Sugden's name's been linked with – there are no dogs among them, he chooses the pretty ones. So I suppose she's the local belle, or used to be, "way back when . . ."'

'Right, you're on. I want pix too, of course, but you'd better not take a cameraman – that's too obvious. Get what you can on your own. If they're a bit fuzzy, it adds to the authenticity. But don't bother too much about it if it's difficult. The first essential is to get a good meaty scandal piece.'

'Leave it to me.'

'Keep in touch. If you seem to be on to something, we'll "trail" it a bit – "Sexpot Sugden Gone from Rome – New Romance Beckons?" – that sort of thing. Then we can run it with an intro like: "Despite all efforts to avoid detection, Jack Sugden's new love-nest is known to the *Gazette*". Or "What takes Jack Sugden to northern hide-out?" But we won't do that until we've got the story assembled. How long d'you think, Paul?'

'No idea. Couple of weeks, maybe a month. These folk are cagey, you know. The minute I got to showing a definite interest in Sugden, they clammed up. But the locals chat to some extent – I can soon find out who his close contacts are, wheedle my way into their confidence.'

'Okay, off you go. Best of British.'

Hilleley returned to Connelton, booked a room on an indefinite basis, unpacked, had a good lunch at the firm's expense, then drove to Hotten. There he consulted the files of the local paper in the public library. He spent the evening in the bar at the Feathers but learned nothing. Next day was Sunday. He drove to Beckindale, to the Woolpack. Investigation had shown him that the village's other pub, the Malt Shovel, wasn't so suitable for cosy chat. Amos saw him come in.

'Morning, sir,' he said. 'Missed your train again?'

'Eh?' Hilleley said, for a moment at a loss. 'Oh, I just went to retrieve my car from Leeds.'

'Taken a fancy to the area, have you?'

'That's right.'

'What'll it be, then?' Amos said, poised to go for the whisky dispenser. He too had a good memory.

'Well, let's see, what have you got?' Hilleley enquired, always willing to impress and taking this opportunity to trace the outline of his new character, the author in search of information. He surveyed the bottles behind Amos's head.

'Brandy? Bourbon? Vodka?'

The choice was in fact quite limited. Amos didn't really approve of mixer drinks.

'What about a nice buck's fizz?'

Amos was peeved. 'If you're willing to pay for the whole bottle of champagne, I can oblige,' he replied. Cheeky article! He'd thought he wouldn't know how to make a buck's fizz.

'That would be a little extravagant, wouldn't it? Us poor authors . . .'

Authors? Amos was about to leap in with an enquiry and an acknowledgement that he too was an author when the door burst open and an eager crowd from the church congregation came surging in. Jack Sugden made it first to the bar. 'Set 'em up, Amos!' he cried, after the style of a Western cattleman. 'Two bitters and an apple juice – '

'Don't be cheeky,' his grandfather chided. 'Cider, Amos.'

Henry appeared almost at once, other customers called for service, and both men became busy. When Amos next thought to pay attention to the newcomer, he found he was at the bar standing next but one to Jack Sugden, apparently engrossed in sampling the local ale. Amos now had two reasons to be disappointed: he hadn't had a chance to chat to the man about his writing, and he'd lost the opportunity to sell some expensive spirits. But the bar was full, he had no time to think about it. Nor did he take note of the fact that Hilleley only stayed as long as the Emmerdale folk. When they went out and clambered into the Land-Rover, Hilleley finished his drink, followed them out, lounged in the forecourt until they had gone, and then went to make his way in search of lunch. He wouldn't have dreamed of contenting himself with a ploughman's at a pub. He went to the

Feathers, had three good courses and a brandy, then drove back to Beckindale.

He had bought an Ordnance Survey map of the district. He pinpointed the old abbey where Sharon Crossthwaite had been killed, and without too much difficulty found the footpath leading to it. The sun shone pleasantly down. But once he got into the pine woods the air struck chill, there was a sombre feeling to the place. He walked on, thinking it was a pity he couldn't find the Crossthwaite family in the local directory; it appeared they had moved out.

Judy Westrop was out for a walk that Sunday afternoon. She had spent the morning helping her father to pack, feeling all the time a little treacherous at not going with him to Wales. After lunch Maurice had elected to sort out his papers; glad of an excuse to get out, Judy had said she wouldn't do any more packing until he was there to supervise. Chance took her to Abbey Woods.

She became aware of the footsteps quite soon after she entered the dark shade of the pine trees. They startled her. She had never come across anyone else taking this particular walk. She paused, more scared than she would have liked to admit, for the place was far from the village and any cry for help would have been wasted. But when the footsteps went on after she paused, she was satisfied she wasn't being followed. And when she came out to the abbey ruins, the man she saw looked quite ordinary, if a little well-dressed by Beckindale standards, in a safari suit of dark blue denim.

'It's all right,' Hilleley said as she hesitated at the edge of the woods. 'I'm not a villain – just a sightseer.' He smiled and nodded. Reassured, she advanced. 'You local?'

'If you mean Beckindale, yes. I live nearby, Home Farm.'

'Did you know the Crossthwaite girl?'

'Who?'

'Sharon Crossthwaite.' Hilleley shrugged. 'You haven't lived here long, or you'd know the name. Her body was found here. Or hereabouts.'

Judy shuddered and drew back. What a strange thing for a stranger to talk about! 'You mean . . . she was murdered?'

'Don't look so scared,' he replied, with a broad grin. 'The feller that did it was caught – he's still in jail.'

'Oh.' She studied him. What was he doing here? A policeman, reopening the case? But he didn't look like a policeman – though these days it wasn't so easy to tell as it used to be. Was he some weirdo, who got his kicks from visiting the scene of murders?

He supplied the answer. 'I'm doing a book on murders and their settings. This is part of the research. Moving round the country, to see what makes a particular place the site of a particular kind of murder.'

Judy gave another little shiver. 'That's gruesome!'

'It's very interesting. Jack the Ripper operated in the East End of London. There were those strange "witch killings" in East Anglia. More recently, the Yorkshire – ' He broke off. Perhaps that wasn't a particularly happy choice of conversation between himself and a pretty girl, alone in the middle of nowhere. 'Shall I walk you through the woods, to save you further alarm? That's if you're going to walk on?'

'Well, I don't intend to stay here all day,' she riposted, and was at once sorry for the sharpness of her tone. 'I'm going down to Beckindale, if you're going that way.'

They made their way through Abbey Woods, not exactly side by side but certainly together. Since he was a stranger in the neighbourhood she acted as guide when they got to Beckindale, showed him the church and the post office and pointed out the trout pools in the river. By and by it seemed only civilized to invite him back for a cup of tea.

Her father greeted the visitor abstractedly and excused himself as soon as he'd drunk one cup, to go in search of a missing day book. Judy refilled Hilleley's cup.

'This seems a big place,' he said. 'It's your father's, is it?'

'Oh, no! He only manages it. And won't, for much longer. On Tuesday he sets out for a new managerial post in Wales.'

'Oh, so I'm lucky to have met up with you then – '

'I'm not going. I shall stay on here.' For a moment she looked a little forlorn, and Hilleley wasn't slow to notice it.

'Going to be lonesome, are you? But not for long, I bet – you've lots of friends around here, I bet.'

'Quite a few.'

'They farm on this scale?' he enquired. It would help if he could get some background on rich farmers – Sugden presumably wasn't living at a lower standard than the Westrops, so it would all add gloss to his feature article.

'Oh, no, N.Y. Estates is much the biggest landowner hereabouts. The others are quite small by comparison.'

'Small?' he asked, perplexed. 'They *look* big.'

She laughed. 'You're a writer, aren't you? Do you always write this kind of documentary book?'

He nodded.

'Never written a novel?'

'I've no time for fiction. Making up stories is child's play – any fool can do it.'

'You'd better not let Jack Sugden hear you say that.'

'Jack Sugden?' he repeated, as if the name was new to him. 'Didn't he write – '

'*Field of Tares* – yes. He lives up at Emmerdale, one of the farms I've just been talking about.'

'He doesn't!'

'He does.'

'I thought he lived abroad – Italy?'

'Not any more. He's back, working on the family farm.'

'Working on it?' Hilleley said, astounded.

'It's a working farm. Cows and sheep. You sound surprised. What did you expect?'

'But . . . what does he know about it?'

'He was born here. He was brought up to it.'

'Yes, but – why should he do it? Why should he do a farmer's job?'

'You'd have to ask him that,' she said demurely. 'All I know is, he seems to have a knack for it.'

'You've seen him at it? I mean, he actually does – what? Milk the cows? Herd the sheep?'

'And mend the walls, and stack the fertilizer, and feed the hens – yes.'

Hilleley was struck dumbfounded. What on earth was whizzkid Jack Sugden up to, getting calluses on his hands doing manual labour? Must be a reason for it. Could he be hiding from someone or something? Or what about the local Venus he had had an affair with – was he setting up a smokescreen so he could see her again?

But it was a bit much, actually becoming a son of the soil, just so as to pick up an old love affair. It was a bewildering turn of events. And one thing was sure, it would take some time to get to the bottom of it.

But with the help of this very attractive girl, who seemed to be on friendly terms with Jack and the rest of the Sugden family, Hilleley had no doubt he'd be able to dig all the dirt out in the end. 'Doing anything this evening?' he enquired.

'What? Well, nothing special. I was going to cook a meal for my father and me.'

'Would he mind eating alone? I thought it might be nice if you and I had dinner at my hotel.'

'Oh, I . . .'

'Please, say yes. It would be a thank-you for the way you came to my aid today – showing me the path back to Beckindale, giving me tea . . . And besides, I'll be all alone otherwise.'

She was tempted, he could see that. 'My father is expecting – '

'Check with him, then, see what he says.'

Maurice was quite keen to get rid of Judy. He found she bothered him, trying to help with his winding up of affairs at Home Farm. When she protested, 'But what about dinner?' he said thankfully that he'd rather get himself a sandwich and a beer when he felt like it. Thus encouraged, Judy accepted Paul Hilleley's invitation to dinner.

She was quite unguarded in her talk to him. When his skilful questions drew her out about the Sugdens, she answered without reserve. But he found she was no help over the matter of Pat Merrick. The name was quite unknown to her.

So though he had every intention of keeping in touch with Judy Westrop, he would have to find other methods of learning the facts about the love affair of long ago.

He drove her home quite early and said a friendly but polite good night. On his way back towards Connelton, he saw a light still on in the Woolpack, though it had just closed at ten. He wondered how to get on close terms with the two men who owned it. Clearly it was Jack Sugden's local, from the way he'd fitted in at lunch-time. Henry Wilks and Amos Brearly must know almost all there was to know about Jack Sugden. But Henry had struck him as being rather a shrewd type. He might do better with Amos, once he set his mind to it.

Amos had just gone to bed. The light downstairs glowed over Henry and Joe Sugden. Joe had come to talk to Henry about the prospect of his visit to the States.

Over the last couple of days, this had somehow become more likely. During this evening, Ed Hathersage had rung again, urging him to make the trip, relating to him the programme of travel he had mapped out for them. Turning away from the telephone, Joe had found his brother's eye upon him.

'I don't know what you're afraid of,' he said. 'Go! You've got the chance, take it!'

'It's not that I'm afraid,' Joe protested. 'I'm anxious, more like. I want to be sure everything will go on all right while I'm away.'

'No one is indispensable,' Jack said, but with a smile that took the sting from the words. 'We'll manage. I'll do the donkey work while Matt keeps an eye on me.'

Joe had looked at Matt for his opinion. Matt nodded slightly and shrugged. Joe's grandfather put in his word without being asked. 'Can't think why you want to go but if you want to, why not?'

'Ma?' Joe enquired.

Annie was thinking that to have Jack fully involved with the farm was a way to make sure he stayed. 'I think we'd manage,' she murmured.

'I'd better ask Henry . . .'

'Henry? What's Henry got to do with it? He doesn't do anything on the farm except lend a hand at harvest,' Old Sam said with heat.

'He's got money invested here as much as any of us,' Joe replied. 'He has a right to say whether I can go.'

So there he was, sitting with Henry over a glass of beer and explaining how he felt about the proposed trip. 'I want to go, I really do,' he said. 'But I couldn't be easy in my mind if I thought owt was going wrong back home while I was living it up in America.'

'Dunno that you'll be living it up so much,' Henry mused. 'From what you tell me, Ed is going to drag you round like a water-skier, in ever-increasing loops. You certainly ought to know more about farming when you get back than you did when you left!'

'It'd be valuable – I know it would be valuable,' Joe said, half-eager and half-unwilling. 'It's a chance I might never get again, to find out how ideas first get put into practice. But sitha, Henry – '

'You don't know if you can trust Jack. That's it, isn't it?'

'Trust him . . . I don't know if that's it, exactly. I think he really wants to do this, to prove himself – prove *to* himself and us that there's summat in him besides mere words. But I don't know that I want to see Emmerdale used as the proving ground.'

Henry sipped his whisky and gave it some thought. 'Jack was brought up to it,' he said in the end. 'He's a farmer's son. Some time or other he must have done most of the things you do. I can't see why he should not be able to do it now.'

'It's not yesterday our Jack left farming. It's over a dozen years gone – I think it's nearly fourteen.'

'What you learn when you're young stays with you longest. I can recite poems I learned in junior school, word for word – with more accuracy than I can tell you what I read in last week's newspaper.'

'Aye, but we're not talking of poetry, Henry. If it were poetry – words – I'd have no qualms about handing over to Jack. It's t'sheer graft of it – the hard physical work. Jack's soft now.'

Henry nodded. 'But not as soft as he was when he first came home. I saw him this morning, catching a ewe and humping her back to Matt for an injection – he couldn't have done that when he first arrived. He's hardening up – and he's willing, Joe! That's the important bit! You could hire a man, if you could spare the cash, to replace yourself. But you'd never hire a man who's as keen as Jack to do everything that's asked of him, and more.'

'You're right there . . .'

'Why not let him have the chance? Matt will be here, keeping control. Your mother has a good head on her shoulders when it comes to the day-to-day business side. Your grandfather is always ready to do what he can – stand-in for milking and so forth. And me too – I know I'm not much cop as a farm-hand, but I'll make sure no silly actions are taken, that you'd disapprove of. All we have to do is keep the place ticking over – right?'

'But it'll soon be the busiest time of the year – '

'True, but the pleasantest time, too. I'd have less enthusiasm about Jack sticking with it if we were heading into a cold, wet winter.'

'Aye,' Joe said with rueful understanding.

'You'll never stop kicking yourself if you don't!'

'Mmmm . . .'

'Where Ed is, the time's still mid-afternoon, Joe . . .'

'You mean, ring him now?'

'Well, you'll have to ring him some time, if you're going.'

'I . . . I believe I will. Can I use your phone?'

'Feel free. But for Pete's sake ask how much the call has cost, so I can put the money in the kitty. Amos will go spare otherwise.'

So while Amos slept peacefully in his bed, his telephone was used for that unheard-of thing, a transatlantic call.

He was told about it next morning. It astounded him so much that he forgot to watch the eggs he was timing, and they came out horribly hard-boiled.

'On my telephone?' he repeated in horror. 'To America?'

'It's what telephones are for, Amos – communication.'

'Not communications with America, Mr Wilks!' But then the import of what he had heard struck home. 'He's going, then?'

'Aye, all fixed up. He's going to arrange a flight today – hopes to take off on Friday.'

'Dear me,' Amos said in amazement. And then, taking

the matter a stage nearer home, 'I suppose it means you'll be spending even more time on Emmerdale business than ever?'

'I'll try not to fall short in my duties as partner, Amos.'

'It would be very inconvenient if you did, Mr Wilks. Just at present, as you know, I have matters of my own as needs my attention.'

'Really? What's that?'

'My horticultural activities.'

'Oh aye. The allotment.'

'I have to be frank with you, Mr Wilks. That piece of land is going to take up some of my attention during the next few weeks.'

'Few years, more like,' Henry said with some sympathy. 'I had a stroll past there when I went birdwatching Saturday afternoon. It's nowt but a tip, Amos.'

'I should have known,' Amos said, digging crossly into his hard egg. 'There was summat about Seth when he told me he'd fixed up for me to have it. And him and Sam Pearson were grinning from ear to ear when they gave me the plan of the allotments to show which were mine.'

'The best thing would be to give them best, then,' Henry suggested. 'It'll half-kill you, having to dig that.'

'That's just what they want,' Amos said, wagging his eggspoon. 'They want to see me look silly – as if that was likely! They think I don't know how to run an allotment.'

'And do you?'

Amos hesitated. 'Well, it isn't in a publican's nature to be gardening, Mr Wilks. I wouldn't have thought of it but for the need to get supplies of really fresh vegetables to ensure our mineral deposits.'

'Mineral deposits? Oh, you mean intake of things like iron and so forth – but we can get all that in spinach and stuff we buy from t'shop.'

'You know as well as I do, Mr Wilks, that every minute a vegetable exists after it's been gathered, lowers the mineral and vitamin content. I'm not saying Ada's vegetables are withered, but lettuces from my own allotment are bound to be better.'

Henry looked as if he didn't quite agree with that, but wisely held his tongue.

'I been doing some reading,' his partner went on. 'About horticulture. Very interesting it is. Digging's an art, Mr Wilks – did you know that?'

'I know it gives you a pain,' Henry said, recalling some digging he'd done for a pretty widow recently arrived in a house in Demdyke Row. 'Some modern art gives you a pain too, so maybe there's a parallel.'

'An art and a science,' Amos said, looking at his buttered toast dreamily. 'I've made a plan, I know just how I'm going to tackle it. But for the first few days, while I do the digging, I may be a bit less attentive to the affairs of the Woolpack.'

'You're never going to dig that in a few days,' Henry said. 'Need a cultivator, more like.'

'Well, er, ahem,' Amos muttered. He bit his toast and munched for a moment. 'Matter of fact, I've hired a mini-cultivator. Break the back of the job, like. But there's rubbish lying about on t'surface that'd break the tines of the machine so I have to clear that first. Then afterwards I have to get a good deep tilth – '

'Tilth?' Henry echoed with appreciation.

'But it won't be quite such hard going after the cultivator's broken up the ground. Howsomever, I'm asking for your aid and co-operation on this, Mr Wilks. It's not often I feel I might fall short, but during the next few days you may have to take more upon yourself than you've been accustomed to. It won't be too much for you?'

'I think I can bear it, Amos.'

'I appreciate that. Aye, all the more so because it's giving me the chance to show them two plotters that I can grow radishes as good as theirs.'

'A worthy aim. In support of that, I'd even undertake to open the new barrel when it's wanted.'

'There's no need to go mad, Mr Wilks,' Amos said in haste. 'Some things still need to be left to the expert.'

During the next few days the other allotment holders were treated to the sight of the landlord of the Woolpack learning to handle a cultivator. The thing ran amok at first, nearly wreaking havoc on the next-door patch, but luckily Amos shut off the little motor in time to stop it dead and overturn it on his own foot. When he hopped about in momentary agony, one of the audience began to whistle mockingly. Amos righted his cultivator, re-read the instruction booklet, and began again.

In ten minutes he had scarified his plot. He was rather annoyed that he'd had to pay a whole afternoon's hire for the cultivator. He sat down to survey his kingdom and was rather impressed by what he had done. When the man from the farmers' co-op came to reclaim the cultivator he too stood a moment in silent tribute.

'Had a cyclone hit you?' he enquired.

'Eh? You what? No, t'weather's been quite good,' Amos said.

'Oh,' said the vanman, and took away the mini-cultivator.

Perhaps because he was so engrossed in his horticulture, Amos almost missed out on the going-away party for Joe Sugden. He was in the bar a little less than usual, and often when he was there he'd be reading a textbook on the culture of vegetables. So he woke with a start one evening to find a conversation in progress that was very interesting.

'I have to change at Kennedy Airport,' Joe was saying. 'Then it's a domestic flight to South Dakota. Ed's meeting me there with a camper, which I think is a sort of glorified minibus – any road, it's to be our home while we dash around from place to place the first week.'

'Sounds efficient,' Jack replied.

'Oh, it was t'travel firm did all the work. I just had to queue up a little while in the consulate in Liverpool for the visa. Nowt to it.'

Kennedy Airport? Visa? All of a sudden Amos was aware that Joe Sugden was on the point of taking off for foreign parts.

'What day is that, again, Joe?' he asked, as if he had been keeping close track of his plans.

'Friday. Take-off's eleven a.m.'

'Can't abide aeroplanes,' Sam Pearson remarked. 'I know

you have to take 'em to get anywhere nowadays, but I always say – '

'If the Almighty had meant men to fly, he'd have given them wings,' Joe and Jack ended in chorus.

'You can laugh. It's true all the same. Seems against nature, dashing through the air in a long tube o' metal.'

'Never mind, Grandad, it isn't you as has to do it this time, it's me. I'm quite excited about the whole thing. Never flown before.'

'A good stiff brandy before you go on board,' Henry advised. 'That's best for pre-take-off nerves.'

'And speaking of that – everybody's invited to my farewell party here tomorrow evening.'

Amos had actually intended to ask Henry to stand in for him on that evening, so that he could get to stage three of his horticultural plan. But he was quite willing to leave the deep digging for another evening.

He was glad he had done so when he saw the crowd that gathered to give Joe a send-off. Everybody was there – even including that chap that kept pottering around Beckindale, the one Judy Westrop seemed to have taken a shine to. Judy was going to feel it badly, Joe's going away. Amos had a shrewd suspicion she'd stayed on in Beckindale after her father left, simply to be near Joe. And now Joe was taking off on an extended visit to the States. Hardly chivalrous of him – but then, Amos suspected, there was more feeling on Judy's side than on Joe's.

All the Emmerdale family were there, and Richard Anstey with a party from N.Y. Estates, and Seth Armstrong with his shy little wife, and the postman, and Ada from the shop, and the fellows who made up the cricket team, and a few from the Young Farmers' Club in Hotten, and a score of others Amos could hardly put a name to.

The only one missing was Dolly.

'How is she, Matt?' Amos asked in a quiet moment.

'Getting along well, I think,' Matt said. 'This new place she's gone to seems ideal. Very quiet, lovely gardens – she seems to spend a lot of time out of doors, with a group of them, like, just talking over things.'

'Sounds very nice,' Amos said, baffled. It didn't sound like medical treatment to him. And besides, what was supposed to be wrong with Dolly? But the doctors knew best, it was to be hoped.

Sam appeared at the bar, asking for a soft drink to replace the half of cider which was all he ever allowed himself. 'How's the allotment?' he enquired.

'Oh, well up to schedule. I'm giving the ground a rest today.'

'And yourself?'

'Eh?'

'A rest. I see you've gone down one spit in your digging. You've more to do.'

'Ah aye, would have been doing it this evening but couldn't miss the do for Joe.' Amos poured the bitter lemon into a glass for Sam. 'I'm not avoiding the hard work, tha knows. I find it very satisfying. And when I think of all the veg I'm going to get – '

Sam raised his eyebrows as he accepted the glass. 'You're sure you'll get 'em, are you? Even the best gardeners can't take that for granted.'

'Oh, but with this modern scientific plan – '

'Huh! Scientific!'

'It's well researched,' Amos assured him with dignity. 'With this deep bed method I'll be getting twice as much return for half the effort.'

Sam gave a grunt of mirth. 'Yon's a fairy tale, lad. Where did you hear it?'

'If you kept up with these things, Sam Pearson, instead of going on all the time the way your father did and his father afore him – like thinking God never intended air travel . . .'

'What's air travel got to do wi' it?'

To tell the truth, Amos didn't quite know. 'It's scientific, like deep bed cultivation,' he explained quickly. 'A system developed over centuries and recently analysed by agricultural researchers. Used in China, it were – '

'In China?' Sam interrupted. 'What you goin' to grow then, rice?'

'An' it were used in France. Aye, France, which is famous for its fine food. You dig deep, and after you've done it you mustn't tread on t'soil.'

Jack, appearing at this moment to make sure his grandfather was being looked after, heard the last remark. 'What's so special about it then?' he enquired.

'You grow twice as much in the same space – that's what,' Amos said in triumph. 'Twice as much and twice as good. It's biodynamic, that's t'secret.'

'And with stereophonic sound, I suppose,' Jack said, laughing. 'Another half, Amos.'

Amos turned to pull the beer. Jack shook his head in amusement.

But Sam Pearson, like Queen Victoria, was not amused. It had suddenly occurred to him that for once Amos might know what he was talking about. It was true, Sam hadn't read a book on horticulture since he was about twenty years old. Things had changed a dickens of a lot since then. How if Amos knew something that Sam did not? And might produce better results?

Judy Westrop had at last got the chance to sit next to Joe for a moment. 'You're all packed, I suppose?'

'Not a bit. I'm going to chuck it all into a case tomorrow morning.'

'I hope you have a wonderful time.'

'Thanks, I'm looking forward to it.'

'You'll write to me?'

'Of course – send you a postcard!'

That wasn't what she had meant, and something of her feelings must have shown momentarily in her eyes. Joe said: 'You'll be all right, eh? Made plenty of other friends in Beckindale by now.'

'Oh, dozens.' She glanced across the room where, through the smoke and the crowds, Paul Hilleley could be glimpsed taking part in a darts match with some of the villagers. He gave a little wave of the hand in acknowledgement when their glances met.

All at once Joe was uneasy. Hilleley was a man he'd only exchanged a dozen words with, but he hadn't taken to him.

He'd heard folk mention that Judy was friendly with him but he hadn't had time to consider it until now.

And now it was too late. He was off to America in the morning. Besides, what could he say? 'Mind yourself when you're with that man, he's a phoney'? Even if the fellow was putting on some kind of an act with his claim to be a writer, that was no reason to take against him.

Joe really meant to get round to having a chat with Hilleley before the evening was over. But there were so many anxious to shake his hand and wish him well that he forgot. Even if he had remembered, he would have got nowhere with him. Hilleley wasn't after Judy Westrop. He had a different target in his sights.

Tomorrow Joe would be gone. And from then on, for a few weeks, Jack would be in charge at Emmerdale Farm.

Chapter Six

Hilleley had watched with avid interest the comings and goings of Jack Sugden, but he was still uncertain whether Jack was even aware that Pat Merrick was in the area.

In this, he underestimated the grapevine that ran among and between the villagers. Of course there had been 'old friends' in the Woolpack or at Hotten Market who were eager to say to him 'I see Pat Merrick's back, eh?'

To which Jack would reply politely, 'So I hear.'

He seemed to be busy about his work on the farm. Hilleley, spying on him from the slopes of Grey Top, saw him trudging about with tools, driving a tractor, struggling with great stones to rebuild a dyke, and half-believed the man simply fell into bed with exhaustion every night.

But Jack was thinking about Pat Merrick. So much so that he got his suitcase down from the top of his wardrobe, opened it, and from it took a folding photograph frame. There were two pictures in the frame; one was of his mother, taken one Harvest Supper when she was laughing as she served the men at long trestles out of doors. The other was of his grandfather, stiff and unbending in his good suit, taken at the time that the fellow survivors of his regiment had held a get-together.

From the back of the frame, between picture and leather, Jack extracted a folded piece of paper. When he opened it out, primary colours leapt to view. It was a child's painting, done in poster paints. It showed a field with sheep, a shepherd (clearly identifiable by his crook) herding them, and a collie on the far side on the alert.

Nothing special in it. Only a daub by a child. But it had life, vitality, and a sense of structure. It was by Jackie Merrick, Pat Merrick's elder child, done when he was six years old.

Jack sat for a time with the painting on the bed at his side. Then, with a sigh, he put it with a pile of magazines and newspapers on his bedside table. He didn't have time to sit here day-dreaming – he was due in Hotten to collect anti-toxin for a sick heifer.

Driving back, he came across Henry Wilks standing by the roadside looking flummoxed. Jack drew up and leaned out. 'Summat wrong, Henry?'

'Nay, not with me. But look here, Jack.' Jack got out and joined him on the grass verge by the wall. Henry pointed with his shooting-stick. A dead woodpigeon lay half-way down the wall of the ditch.

'Aye?' Jack said. 'Somebody been out shooting?'

'It's not been shot, Jack. That's the third I've seen today. I've been out birdwatching so I was in Verney's Woods – there was one there, and one by Carron Cross, and now this.'

'Old birds, happen?'

'No, average – and not starved either – in fact the one I saw up by Carron Cross had a full crop!'

They stared down at it for a moment. Then Henry took from his pocket the plastic tin in which he'd carried a sandwich lunch. He stooped and put the dead pigeon in it.

'What's that for, Henry? Pigeon pie?'

'I don't fancy eating this one, Jack. Because it's not been shot, and it hasn't died of malnutrition. Which seems to leave only one thing.'

Jack frowned. 'Aye,' he said. 'As it happens, I've just seen Stokes, been getting some stuff for Laurell II. He said he'd call round later today, see if everything was all right.'

'Good. We'll show him this.'

'Want a lift down to the village?'

'Nay, I'll walk – see if I spot owt else. Thanks all the same, Jack.'

After Jack had driven off, Henry turned back over the wall and across the fields. He was skirting a field of knee-high wheat when he came across Richard Anstey standing by a stile, making notes on a pad.

'Looks good, does it?' Henry asked.

'Coming along well. New strain – we might plant more of it next year. Well, Henry, seen any flamingoes or golden eagles?'

'I once saw a flamingo,' Henry said. 'Nearly gave me a stroke. It had escaped from a wildlife park.'

'I once saw a green parrot,' Anstey rejoined. 'Eating wild crab apples in Hotten Park. But that turned out to be an escapee too.'

Henry fetched the sandwich box out of his anorak pocket and opened it. 'What d'you make of this, Anstey?'

'A pigeon. Nothing very unusual, I'm afraid.'

'Take another look. Not been shot.'

Anstey poked the bird with his forefinger. 'What are you saying? That it's poisoned?'

'Well, I found this one by the road on t'way to Emmerdale, and another I saw was in your big woods, and there was a third elsewhere.'

Anstey gave the bird another prod. 'Not starved. Quite the opposite – I'd say it was gorged.'

'Aye. I'm showing it to John Stokes this afternoon.'

'That's not a bad idea. And I'll tell you something else that's worth mentioning to him. I saw a funny thing the other afternoon. I was walking in the plantation and this fox came walking towards me.'

'In broad daylight?'

'Aye!'

'Walking – not dashing past you?'

'Didn't have an ounce of fear in him. He stood and looked at me, turned, and walked away. Walked, not ran, Henry.'

'That's really strange.'

'The thing seemed in a dream. Dazed, you know? Still, that's not the point, really. Nothing to do with poisoned pigeons.'

'Unless the fox had eaten one,' Henry said.

They looked at each other in perplexity. 'Mmmm . . .' said Anstey. 'But who uses that kind of stuff these days?'

It was a mystery.

In the afternoon Matt went to see Dolly at the convalescent home. She was in the second week of her stay, would be coming home on Saturday. Annie was already bustling about doing extra cleaning to make sure the place looked attractive, and had baked Dolly's favourite cake as a celebration. Jack did minor chores around the farmyard, waiting for the arrival of Mr Stokes, who would look at Laurell II and advise about the delivery of Campion's calf, expected any moment now.

Henry arrived as Stokes was finishing his examination of Campion. 'She should be okay, Jack, but I'll drop by again this evening – I'm off out to Petby to dose a herd of pigs so it'll take me a while. Afternoon, Henry,' he added as Henry looked in on them.

'Finished in here, John?'

'Aye, just let me sluice off.' The vet ran cold water from the tap over his hands, shook them vigorously, and pulled paper towels off the big roll Jack held for him.

'I'd like you to take a look at this,' Henry said, holding out the box with the pigeon.

Puzzled, Stokes accepted the box. When he'd looked inside he seemed no wiser. 'I don't generally get asked to resuscitate woodpigeons,' he joked.

'Can you tell what's wrong with him?'

'He's dead, Henry, very dead.'

But Henry refused to joke about it. 'What did he die of?'

Stokes looked at him, and then the smile died on his round features. 'Ah,' he said. 'See what you mean.'

'I mustn't influence your judgement but . . .'

'You think it's poisoned?'

'Yes, I do. And I'll tell you something else. I think it was this that did it.' Henry dipped his hand into his jacket pocket and came up with a plastic bag twisted into a knot. He undid it and poured out on to the palm of his other hand a few seeds of barley.

'You what?' Stokes said.

'I saw another dead bird up along Ernest Tolly's fields. That was after Richard Anstey told me he'd seen a groggy fox in N.Y.'s plantation. Tolly's land runs almost alongside that plantation so that's why I went there. He's late this year, sowing – some of it is springing now but some is just lying on the surface and this dead bird, the last one I saw, was lying among a scattering of seed that hadn't germinated. I just thought I'd gather up a few of 'em. Seems funny – all the dead pigeons are on the perimeter of Tolly's patch, and the fox was hard by where he could catch poisoned birds.'

Jack's dark features began to take on a flush of indignation. 'Are you saying that Ernie Tolly has been putting out poisoned seed to kill pigeons?'

'I've no idea, Jack. All I know is there are four dead birds round his land, and one of 'em was lying right in the middle of this seed.'

'I'll take it, Henry,' said the vet. He accepted the polythene bag with its contents. 'I'll examine the bird and the seed, see if I can find any connection. But I can hardly believe it. Nobody uses toxic poisons these days. Or if they do, it's under strictly controlled conditions.'

'Oh aye?' Henry said. 'Remember Geoff Atwill and the dog violets, Jack?'

'Of course. Somebody using chemical weedkiller.'

'That was on the roadside bank near Tolly's farmland.'

'By heaven,' Jack exclaimed, 'if he's spreading stuff like that around, he wants his head examined.'

The surge of protective anger surprised him. He felt that Emmerdale was endangered by the carelessness of some foolhardy outsider, and the thing he wanted more than anything else at that moment was to be able to set up some kind of protective barricade, to save his land from harm. *His* land! But it didn't belong to him. It was the property of Emmerdale Farm Limited, and if anyone could claim rights over it it was his younger brother.

On the Saturday, Matt went to fetch Dolly home from the nursing home. Annie was surprisingly bothered about the homecoming. She kept going to the window to watch out for the car.

'We should have put up a bit of bunting, happen?' Jack suggested in amusement.

'Nay, that'd be the worst thing. It's been ever so quiet and restful at that place. It'll be a big change, now she's home.'

'I'd hardly call this the hub of commerce, Ma. Emmerdale's quiet enough.'

'Yes, but . . .'

They heard the car turn into the yard. She flew to the door to open it. Matt was helping Dolly out. Annie went across to give her a kiss on the cheek – a gesture of affection so unusual that Jack raised his eyebrows.

'Lovely to have you home again, love.'

'Lovely to be home, Ma.'

'Come inside. It's muddy standing here – '

'It's all right, I'm not made of bone china, you know.' But Dolly followed her in, looking about alertly at the old farm kitchen. 'Eeh, I missed this,' she murmured.

'Welcome home,' Jack said. 'I know just how you feel.'

'Do you?' She gave him a sudden, piercing glance.

Jack was startled. He'd been thinking of her as a convalescent, perhaps a little weak and slow. But there was a quickness in her manner that told him something very different – Dolly was very keyed up.

'Now, after we've eaten,' Annie said, ushering her to a chair, 'you must have a nap, and then we'll have tea about – '

'A nap?' Dolly shook her head, laughing. 'I've had enough sleeping and resting to last me the rest of my life. Nay, I'll tell you what I'm going to do this afternoon – I'm going to Hotten.'

'Hotten?' Annie echoed, amazed. This wasn't the way invalids were supposed to behave.

'I've been planning it for days. You just can't imagine how dull it's all been – and it's three weeks since I saw a bit of life. Time to get going again. So I'm going to buy a new dress in celebration.'

Sam had come forward to give her a hug. She spoke these words across his shoulder. He set her away from him and gazed at her face. 'Are you sure you're up to jaunting about – '

'Oh, I'm fine, Grandad, really, fine. And if that's dinner that smells so good, I'm famished!'

During the meal she seemed sprightly – too sprightly, perhaps. Jack caught his mother turning a worried gaze on her from time to time when she was talking with too much animation. Matt, too – from time to time he put his hand over hers, as if to calm and reassure her. Between them they gently tried to dissuade her from going to Hotten that afternoon, but she was as determined as they were. She won in the end, though Matt had pointed out that they wouldn't get back in time for milking.

'Oh, Jack and Grandad can do it,' she pointed out. 'Jack's learned a lot about farming since he got back, haven't you, Jack?'

'I've learned that I'd forgotten a lot,' he admitted. 'Mostly, what hard work it is.'

'But you don't complain, do you?' she said quickly. 'You do your stint – Matt says you pull your weight and more, since Joe went.'

'That's kind of him,' Jack said. He smiled at Matt. 'I feel it's an accolade.'

'Accolade, what's that?' Matt said, trying to lighten the atmosphere, which had grown strangely tense. 'Some new form of lemonade?'

'Speaking of lemonade,' Sam said, 'shouldn't we have a little drop of summat this evening, to celebrate Dolly's homecoming?'

'Oh, Grandad, that'd be lovely. Down at t'Woolpack – and I can say thank you to Amos for his present – '

'I wouldn't if I were you. He were that embarrassed when he gave it to me, he'll die if you mention it.'

'Well, it'll be lovely to see him again. And Henry too. So I need that new dress, Matt. Come on, eat up, we want to get going.'

There was nothing to be done about it – go they must, unless Matt wanted to put his foot down. And from the way Dolly was acting, that would end in a flood of tears.

She insisted on helping with the washing of the dishes before she and Matt set off. Jack had gone out to look for some of Annie's poultry, which had gone a-wandering. Sam sat in his chair, alone with his daughter. She sat down with some knitting, to listen to a play on radio. After a bit Sam moved restlessly.

She looked up. 'I thought you'd be out in your garden, Dad.'

'Should be . . . Or watching the cricket – Hotten Agricultural College against Connelton High School . . .'

'What's the matter?'

'Eh, lass.' She was surprised to see the glint of tears in his old eyes. 'I were just thinking . . . Two grandsons but no great-grandchilder. I thought by now to have seen little 'uns toddling about the place.'

'Nay, Dad!' What had brought on this sad look into the family prospects? 'There's plenty of time yet.'

'D'you think so? I'm not getting any younger, and neither Joe nor Jack seems to think of settling down. And even Dolly . . .'

'What about Dolly?'

'She's not likely to have any kiddies now, is she?'

Annie muffled a sigh. 'There's no way of knowing, Dad. But she hasn't had the best of luck, that's true.'

'You know,' her father was continuing, 'there was a lot of talk about Jack and – '

'Now, Dad!'

'Don't "Now Dad!" me! You know what everybody always said about that kiddie. If it's true, then he's a Sugden, not – '

'What d'you want, then? That Jack should claim him,

demand to bring him here? Make him his heir, like?' She gave a little gesture, taking in the kitchen. 'Of all this? Any road, it's all gossip – stuff I don't like to hear – or believe.'

For a few minutes her father was silenced. Then he said: 'It's not as if him or Joe was showing the slightest sign of becoming family men. I don't know what's come to youngsters, these days. At Jack's age I'd recognized my responsibilities but he doesn't even seem to see there's such a thing.'

'But he's made the decision to stay here, Dad – to work, to take his part in the farm.'

'For how long?' Sam said bitterly. 'Fly-by-night, that's him. He always was and he always will be.'

She was about to speak sharply, but checked herself. She understood that the harsh words he was uttering were not really aimed at Jack, but at life itself, for its cruelty towards poor Dolly and for its failure to give Sam Pearson the continuity of his line.

She laid aside her knitting, rose to switch off the radio which had chatted on unnoticed for some time, and went to the Aga to pick up the kettle. 'I'll make us a secret cup of tea, Dad,' she said with a smile. 'You need cheering up.'

'Ah, Annie, don't treat me like a child – '

'It's not that, Dad. But what's to be done about it? My two sons are grown men, they must make their own minds. As to Matt and Dolly, I've had them in my prayers this long while. So now all that's left, Dad, is to make a cup of tea and forget about it.' She laughed, and was rewarded with a weak smile from Sam. 'That's the way. And if it means anything, Dad – I think Jack is beginning to feel a strong bond between himself and Emmerdale.'

'Mmmm . . .' murmured Sam, allowing himself to be comforted. But then, just to show he could also find a dark cloud outside a silver lining, 'And how's our Joe going to take to that, eh, if he has to share control with his brother?'

'Oh, Dad,' Annie said, with half a laugh and half a sigh.

But it might well turn out to be a point of some importance.

When the party from Emmerdale came into the Woolpack

bar that evening, Amos almost disgraced himself by rushing forward to greet them. But luckily he couldn't get out from behind the counter because Old Walter was in the way, so his dignity was preserved. Nevertheless, he beamed on Dolly.

'Lass, it's grand to see you,' he said. And indeed, she was a picture, in the new dress of soft flower-dotted lawn. 'Settling in all right, are you?'

'Yes, right glad to be home,' she said. 'And I'd like to thank all the kind friends who sent messages to me in hospital an' all.'

Amos almost blushed. He knew what she meant. He said in haste, 'And what are you having, then?'

He took orders and poured their drinks. He and Henry hovered over them for a time, catching up on the news, not only about Dolly but about Joe. Joe had written, a sketchy letter – 'But then he never was much of a one for writing,' Henry said comfortingly.

'Does anybody know if he's written to Judy Westrop?' Amos enquired.

'She hasn't mentioned it – but there's no reason why she should. Why d'you ask, Amos?'

'She's getting a bit too thick wi' that writer fellow,' Amos said.

'Can't see how you can tell it's "*too* thick",' Henry said. 'How thick is too thick?'

Amos glanced over his shoulder to the spot where Hilleley was playing dominoes with old Tim Darnton. 'What's he want to take up wi' Tim for?' he demanded. 'They've nowt in common, and you know what rubbish Tim talks when he's got a pint and a half inside him.'

'But what's that got to do with him and Judy getting friendly?' Henry insisted.

'It's only . . . I've got an instinct for this sort o' thing, Mr Wilks. Can't be in the licensed trade as long as I have, wi'out developing an instinct, and mine tells me that's a bad 'un.'

Annie looked up with interest from her glass of dry sherry. She took a quick look at Hilleley. It was true, she didn't find him appealing. He seemed to turn up where he wasn't expected, hanging about almost as if he was spying on someone. But then, if he was gathering material for a book about crimes in the area, then happen he did have to lurk about in a way that a farmer or stockman wouldn't.

Hilleley acknowledged defeat at the hands of old Tim Darnton and made his way towards the bar for a refill. Coming back, he had no particular goal, so it was quite natural that he should pass close by. In fact, he seemed to choose a place near them to pause and sip.

Jack turned in his chair and regarded him. Hilleley, under that cool scrutiny, was almost forced to speak. 'Having a sort of celebration, it looks like?' he ventured.

'It's my welcome home,' Dolly said, eager to be friendly.

'In that case, welcome.' He held up his glass to her before he took another sip.

'Thank you.' Dolly was about to add, 'Won't you join us?' but Jack broke in before she could utter the words.

'There's Seth,' he said. 'Come and sit with us for a bit, Seth!'

Seth Armstrong raised a hand in salute, bought a pint from Henry, and came across. Hilleley still lingered, half belonging to their group and half not. All the same there was a feeling of his being all ears to what they said.

'Seth, you seen anything funny among your gamebirds?' Jack said in a carrying tone.

'Funny? In what way?'

'Any of them dropped dead without shotgun pellets to help 'em?'

'Well, it's funny you should say that, but I found a dead pheasant on the edge of the woods day before yesterday.'

'What did you do with it?' Henry said, coming back to join them for a moment. 'You didn't feed it to any of your pointers, did you?'

'Do you think I'm daft?' Seth said. 'You don't feed a game dog on game. Nay, I were going to give it to my missus for us dinners, but somehow I didn't fancy it so I buried it in the compost heap.'

'Just as well,' Henry said. 'Happen it was poisoned.'

'Poisoned? What with?'

'Dunno yet. The vet's still doing tests. Could be it's some kind of pesticide.'

Hilleley had lost interest, and in any case Judy Westrop had arrived. He drifted off to join her. Jack seemed pleased to be rid of him, Annie noticed.

'Did Anstey tell you about that fox he saw?' Henry went on to Seth.

'Aye, he did, and I'll tell you a funny thing! Yesterday afternoon I saw a scatter of hen's feather's in the lane by Carron Cross – they weren't there midday when I went home to my dinner, so that means a fox was out in daylight, and got an easy meal. Could be that one Anstey saw – too sick to hunt properly, just grabs whatever it can get.'

'There goes your missing hen, Ma,' Jack said to Annie.

'Aye. I thought it were funny – that one, I call her Dumpy – she used to stray a lot in the daytime and often would lay in a hedge or roadside, but she always came home at night to roost in her own coop. When she didn't turn up to be shut in, I more or less knew summat had happened to her.'

'It's getting a bit expensive,' Seth remarked, 'whoever's spreading this pesticide about is costing his neighbours a bob or two. One hen, one pheasant – '

'And could have been one Seth, if you'd cooked that pheasant,' Henry said in a grim tone.

'Hey!' said Seth in alarm. 'Don't thee say such things!'

'But it's true, Seth,' Sam pointed out. 'So thee be careful. Don't eat owt that hasn't got a clean bill of health.'

'Nay,' Seth said with a grin, 'I'll wait and have a good feast on the veg from Amos's allotment. How's it coming, Amos?'

To Seth's surprise, Amos responded with a smile of pleasure. 'Ah, there's nowt like it!' he declared. 'Standing there of an evening, looking over your plot, and knowing there's organic activity going on all around you.'

'Organic activity?'

'Aye, the age-old interaction between bacteria and soil elements – '

'Swallowed a dictionary, then, have you?' Sam winked at

Seth. 'But what really counts is knowing what to plant, and looking after it once it's planted – '

'Oh, I've got my seeds in, don't you worry,' Amos rejoined.

'But . . . where did you get 'em? Who did you ask?' Sam was quite vexed. He'd expected to be consulted, as a local expert.

'I got all that out of my book. *Deep Bed Cultivation and Its Product*, a wonderful book, tells you everything. Wi' this no-digging method, you have to be sure you plant vigorous strains – '

'No-digging method? Talk sense, Amos. You can't grow veg without digging.'

'You do it only the once to get the deep bed ready. After that, you don't touch it. You leave it to Nature. Ah, Nature . . . !' rhapsodized Amos, but was called away to serve a customer before he could give Sam and Seth his views on her charms.

'Daft article,' Seth grunted in Sam's ear. 'If he don't dig and hoe, he'll get nowt but a crop of weeds.'

'Happen,' Sam said. But he sounded less certain than Seth. Amos seemed so sure of himself.

Next day, Sunday, they went to church. Dolly was welcomed back by the vicar, Mr Hinton, and greeted by friends from the outskirts of Beckindale who hadn't seen her on the previous day. Annie thought she was too talkative again, but perhaps after being away three weeks she felt she had a lot to catch up on.

On Monday morning, about nine o'clock, Dolly appeared from upstairs looking a little heavy-eyed. 'Morning, love,' said Annie. 'You slept well?'

'Bit too well, I think. I feel all dozy. Where is everybody?'

'Out on the job.'

'What's the time then?' She turned quickly to look at the clock. 'Five past nine! But I asked Matt to give me a nudge when he went downstairs!'

'At six o'clock, Dolly? That would have been silly. 'Sides, he thought you could do with a lie-in – '

'But he knows I wanted to take the half past eight bus to Hotten!'

She made for the outside door. Annie said: 'I'll get you some breakfast – ' and when Dolly hurried out without taking any notice, followed her. Matt was just crossing the yard in search of a can of detergent.

'Matt!' cried Dolly. 'I've missed my bus now!'

'Well, there'll be other buses, love – '

'But I wanted to be in Hotten bright and early – '

'But you were only in Hotten on Saturday afternoon, Dolly.'

'It would've been no good asking after jobs on Saturday afternoon!'

There was a startled pause. Annie, who had been about to ask Dolly if she wanted bacon or what, tactfully drew back into the kitchen again.

'What do you want a job for, love?' Matt asked in a quiet tone.

'I need to have summat to do, Matt.'

'But there's plenty to do on the farm.'

'Oh, aye, but that's not the kind of thing . . .'

'I thought you were enjoying it, learning to milk and to care for orphan lambs and that . . .'

'I did enjoy it, Matt. But it's not a full-time thing – '

'Now Dolly, you don't want a full-time job, surely – '

'Why not? Other women do it.'

'But other women haven't – '

'Just had a miscarriage? Just spent two weeks in the booby hatch?'

He came to her and put an arm round her. 'I didn't mean that, Dolly. Don't put words like that into my mouth.'

'But it's true, isn't it? I'm no good at being a mother, it seems. So I thought I'd better have a bash at being a career woman.'

If he thought it was a little optimistic to expect to become a career woman through a job in Hotten, he didn't say so. He let a moment go by then said, 'If you're in a hurry and don't want to wait for the next bus, Jack's going into Hotten later this morning. Wants to talk to the vet.'

'Oh. I can get a lift with him, you mean?' She had been tensed up for a row. She should have known that Matt never rowed. She looked momentarily nonplussed, even a little ashamed. 'All right then, I'll ask him.'

'I'll ask him. He's up the twenty acre. You go and get summat inside you if you're going marching round Hotten job-hunting.'

'Aye.' She looked up at him, suddenly stood on tiptoe and kissed him with quick gratitude. 'I don't deserve you,' she said, then hurried inside.

In due course Jack drove her to Hotten. They came home in time for the midday meal with something to report on each side. Dolly had been given details of four jobs that interested her, the best being the post of assistant to Huxley, Hotten's chief auctioneer. 'I'll have a read of these information sheets later,' she said, 'and see what I think.'

Annie looked at Matt. He gave a very slight shrug but said nothing. Jack had news from the vet. 'Stokes said he did all kinds of tests and was quite baffled for a bit. He says he found traces of mercury, but was satisfied it wasn't enough to have killed the bird.'

'Mercury?' Sam exclaimed, laying aside his knife and fork. 'No one's using mercuric dressing for seed in this day and age, surely!'

'Well, Stokes says he couldn't believe it was that either. But something kept niggling at the back of his mind – he felt he should recognize the stuff but it wouldn't come to him. But then he recalled a time when he'd done hundreds of tests, all turning up the same results.'

'You say hundreds?' Annie put in, in alarm.

'Aye, Ma, hundreds – woodpigeons mainly, but some pheasants, partridges, rooks, doves, and not just seed-eaters but hawks as well.'

'Jack!' his grandfather said. 'I remember that time! That was years ago, afore we understood the damage stuff like that could do.'

'D'you remember the name of the stuff, Grandad?'

'Hang on a bit . . . Joe would know . . . Den – no, Enidren, that's it. Enidren – it were taken off the market.'

'Used as a seed dressing to prevent fungus diseases in wheat and barley – can still be used under special controls, Stokes says, because properly used it's quite safe. Only now it's being used improperly. And that's what was in that woodpigeon. I stopped by to tell Henry on the way home – he was right put out about it. If you remember, a lot of peregrine falcons were killed last time round.'

'But where's it coming from?' Annie asked. 'Nobody has it these days – I mean, it would be somebody with the resources of N.Y. Estates, and you can be sure Richard Anstey would never let anyone use it without safeguards.'

'It's a mystery,' Jack said, with grim anger, 'but it had better be solved soon before we lose summat more important than Dumpy the hen.'

After dinner Dolly and Annie cleared away. Then, feeling she hadn't exactly pulled her weight today, Dolly volunteered to dust and tidy Jack's room. She came down again half an hour later with a small pile of magazines – *Farmer's Weekly, British Farmer & Stockbreeder, Dairy Management*.

'He takes it seriously, doesn't he?' she remarked. 'Can I put these out for the dustmen, or will he want to keep them?'

'Oh, I think he's finished with them. But just sort through to see if there's any he's marked to keep. He turns them open at the article he wants, if he's specially interested.'

Dolly duly sorted through. And thus it was she who came upon the child's painting.

'Well, look at this, Annie,' she said, pausing.

Annie turned from the sink, where she was preparing a salad for tea, and looked over her shoulder. Dolly heard her draw in a breath.

'What is it?' she asked, turning her head.

She saw Annie had gone a little pale.

'It's a painting by a little boy whose name is always being linked with Jack,' she replied. 'And . . . why should Jack have kept it?'

Chapter Seven

Dolly was too tactful to ask for any further enlightenment. She handed the painting to Annie. 'Happen Jack would like to have it – I shouldn't put it out for the dustmen, should I?'

'No, Dolly. Thank you.' Annie took it and put it in a drawer of the dresser. Dolly finished sorting through the magazines, tied them up, and took them out to the shed. From there it was only a step to the big barn, where Matt was inspecting the silage they had put in last week.

'Matt . . . ?'

'Yes, love?'

'Can I ask you something?'

'What?'

'Who's Jackie Merrick?'

Matt wheeled to look at her. 'What on earth makes you ask that?'

'I just found a child's painting with the name Jackie Merrick lettered on it in pencil. It was among Jack's old magazines. Annie looked as if she'd seen a ghost when I handed it over to her.'

'Aye,' Matt said. 'I can just imagine.'

He came to her, put his arm round her, and they stood in the shade of the oak by the barn. The sun shone through the leaves, making a dappled pattern on the ground and on their shoulders.

'It goes back into the past,' he murmured. 'There was this lass called Pat Harker – '

'Any relation to Mrs Harker at Drygrounds?'

'Her niece. But Pat's family lived in Beckindale in them days. She married a feller called Tom Merrick, a right load of trouble. Was then and still is, as far as I can gather – his name was in t'*Hotten Courier* a couple of weeks ago for being up on a charge of drunk and disorderly.'

'Go on,' she prompted, for Matt had stopped as if two and

two had suddenly made four. He had just realized why it was that Pat and her children had come to stay with Elsie Harker.

'Jackie Merrick is her eldest kid,' he continued. 'He'll be – what? – fourteen or thereabouts now.'

'But this was a child's painting, Matt. A little kiddie's.'

'Aye. Well, when he painted it, I think he was six, mebbe seven.'

'And our Jack still has it?'

'Seems so. I don't know the ins and outs of it. I remember him with a painting – it were on one of his trips home, soon after he'd made a lot o' money with that book of his. Aye,' Matt said, wrinkling his brow, 'I remember him saying he'd bought it, and I said he could get plenty like it for nowt if he just asked the schoolteacher. But he said there was summat special about that one.'

'Special,' Dolly repeated.

'I think what he meant was, he'd paid money for it to help Pat Merrick. She was having a terrible time with Tom, so Jack . . . well, I think he wanted to give her enough money to get away for a new start somewhere. Pat was the kind of lass as wouldn't take a gift of money. So Jack bought the painting, I think.'

'She went away?'

'Leeds or Bradford, I imagine.'

'With her husband?'

'I don't remember the details, love. It's a long time ago. There was a lot o' gossip then, but everybody was always quick to gossip about Jack.'

'Except you, love,' said Dolly. She leaned against him. 'You never gossip, do you?'

'Get on with you! I'm only human. But I don't think there's much good in raking up the past.'

'That's right,' she agreed, but with a shake of the head. 'Yet Jack's kept the painting all this time, eh? And had it out recently, because it was among a bundle of magazines he'd been reading.'

'Poor old Jack.'

'You call him poor?'

Matt smiled at her. 'Well, compared wi' us, he is, isn't he?

No one to call his own, no place he really belongs. Kind o' lonely and lost, he seems to me sometimes. I wouldn't change places with him for all the tea in China.'

Dolly stayed close against his shoulder. All at once she felt a tide of gratitude and happiness rising inside her. She was home again, and with the man she loved. What was all this nonsense about dashing back and forth to Hotten in search of a job? What was she trying to prove? The time might come when she could do something really worthwhile, but for the moment to be insisting on a paid position away from Emmerdale was like punishing Matt for her own failures.

She belonged here, beside Matt. All the rest was fantasy.

Jack came into the kitchen a little too early for the afternoon cup of tea. He wanted to ring one of the neighbouring farmers to ask for the loan of some black polythene. 'What's Barnaby's number, Ma?' he enquired.

'I don't recall it. It's in the notebook.'

He opened the dresser drawer in search of it, and found the painting.

'How did this get here?' he asked.

'You left it among some old newspapers. Dolly brought it down.'

'Oh.'

'You want to keep it?'

'Yes, thanks, Ma.'

A hundred questions crowded to her lips, but she asked none of them. If he wanted to talk, he would do so.

He found the notebook with phone numbers, looked up Barnaby, and dialled. After a bit he replaced the receiver. 'No answer. Ma, there's something I wanted to ask you.'

She braced herself. 'Go on.'

'Do you think Joe would object if I were to buy a couple of pedigree cows for the herd?'

Whatever she had expected, it wasn't that. She almost gasped in surprise, yet managed not to look astounded. Summoning her forces she said: 'Pedigrees?'

'Aye. I've been thinking . . . Matt's been showing me how the milk records are kept and once I'd read the names on the eartags, I've begun to know the cows by name. It's been a bit like the old days, when Dad were alive . . .'

'We had a lot fewer cows in those days, lad.'

'That's right. And those we've got now are a credit to us – I'm not saying otherwise. I understand we're grading-up but we've still got a lot of non-pedigree calves coming along.'

'The idea Joe had, he wanted to get part of the herd pedigree – it takes about three generations of calves starting from scratch.'

'But that's the slow way to build up a pedigree herd?'

'Of course. And you have to have the non-pedigree part to finance the work on the up-grading.'

'Matt says we need to buy in a few really good beasts to get going properly.'

'It'd be quicker, certainly.'

'How long would it take us? If we were to buy?'

Annie smiled. 'How long does it take to grow an oak tree? Depends how much money you put into buying the saplings. Same with cows.'

'No, how long, Ma?'

'Five or six years? About that. But I don't really know about such things. You want to talk to Clifford Longthorn over Lower Hall Farm.'

'I remember Longthorn!' Jack exclaimed. 'Dad had a blazing row with him – at least, t'other way round, when one of Dad's bulls got in among his cows.'

'Fancy remembering that! Aye, it were a right up-and-down. Clifford were particular then and he's a lot more particular now.'

'Friesians, isn't it?'

She nodded.

'How'd it look? "Emmerdale Herd of Pedigree British Friesians" – on a board down the lane. How would Joe feel about it?'

'Why don't you ask him?'

'Bit difficult, him being in Dakota.'

'He told us in his last letter which camp-site they were going to be at this week. Why don't you try ringing him?'

'Ring a camp-site?'

Annie nodded her head at him. For once she knew more about something than Jack did. 'You should hear Ed Hathersage about American camp-sites. They're a bit up on the kind we've got here. They'll have telephones at the office and for all I know phone booths dotted all round the site. One thing's sure – if you ring at a time when Ed and Joe would be back after the day's driving, they'd fetch Joe to the phone.'

'It'd cost a fortune, Ma!' Jack protested.

To his surprise, she laughed. 'What, four or five pounds? When you're talking about buying pedigree cows?'

He hesitated then joined her amusement. 'Aye, it's the Yorkshire in me. Right, I'll set my alarm for the middle of the night so I can ring him about eight in the evening, their time.'

She looked at him, and saw he was serious. 'Jack . . .'

'Yes?'

'Be careful what you say. Cows have always been Joe's concern.'

'You mean, don't let him think I'm trying to step into his shoes the minute he's away.'

'It's not so much shoes as toes, lad. Don't tread on Joe's toes.'

'I'll be the soul of tact.'

'Oh aye? I'd like to hear that,' she said drily.

When he had gone out with Matt after tea, Dolly collected up the cups and saucers. 'About that job, Ma,' she began.

'The one with Huxley's?'

'I've just been telling Matt – I've decided not to pursue it.'

Annie turned with a questioning glance. Dolly carefully put two saucers together so that they fitted and put them handy for Annie to wash. 'It were all a sort of . . . I dunno – I had a fizzy feeling inside me, as if I had to hurry around as fast as ever I could to prove . . . to prove . . .'

'What, lass?'

'That I wasn't round the bend, or inadequate, or summat.'

'Nobody ever thought you were daft, my lass.' Annie smiled at the idea. 'And as to inadequate – '

'I couldn't carry our baby to full term.'

'But that's not uncommon, especially with a first – ' She broke off.

'Aye . . . It wasn't my first, you see.'

'But it's some years since then, Dolly. And women are delicate in some ways. Just because you've had one miscarriage, it doesn't mean you'll have others.' Annie paused. 'I lost a child, you know.'

'You did?'

'Aye, between our Peggy and Joe. So you see, it's not evidence of owt desperately wrong. Joe arrived safe and sound after all.'

Dolly nodded. 'Aye, nobody safer and sounder than our Joe,' she agreed. 'Thank you, Annie, for telling me.'

'Ah well . . . Women's talk, Grandad would call it. And where is he, now I come to speak of him? Never came in for his afternoons.'

'He's out gloating over Amos doing his gardening.'

'Him and Seth,' Annie said in a tone of reproach. 'It'll serve 'em right if Amos grows prize vegetables.'

'No chance of that. Have you happened by his allotment? The weeds are springing up faster than his seeds.'

Annie shook her head and gave her attention to the washing-up.

When Dolly had gone out to collect the eggs, Annie was surprised to hear a car drive into the yard. She looked out, didn't recognize the car, but recognized the man getting out. It was that somehow unlikeable stranger, the writer.

He tapped at the door. She went, wiping her hands. He gave her a polite smile. 'Mrs Sugden?'

'That's right.'

'The name's Paul Hilleley.' He held out his hand. With secret unwillingness, she took it. 'Mind if I come in a minute?'

'Of course.' She ushered him in, still without any impulse of welcome towards him.

'You're the mother of Jack Sugden, the writer?'

'You surely know that by now, Mr Hilleley. You've been in Beckindale a couple of weeks now.'

'That's so. I just like to get my facts right.'

'Is this some business matter to do with Jack?'

'No, it's . . . Er . . . I'm a writer myself, you know, and I'm engaged on a book about the emotional and psychological effects of tragedy – '

'I don't see how Jack – '

'No, no, it was only that I . . . This is to be a serious book, you know. A book about people suddenly confronted by catastrophe – '

'From what I heard, I understood your book was summat to do with murder?'

'Yes, indeed, murder in its setting – its effect on the family, the friends . . . You, I believe, were once stricken by the loss of a member of your family?'

Annie frowned. What could he mean? Tragic loss summoned up the death of Peggy – from purely natural causes – and her twins – in an accident. Nothing about murder. Her instinctive dislike of the man suddenly rose in her. 'Everybody has experienced loss at some time in their life, Mr Hilleley. It'd be much better if you'd come to the point instead of making pretty speeches!'

Hilleley was taken aback at her bluntness, but summoned a laugh. 'Spoken like a true Yorkshirewoman, Mrs Sugden. You don't mince words!'

'I've better things to mince. Say what you want, Mr Hilleley.'

'I was speaking to the landlord of the inn . . . Mr Brearly . . .'

'Oh aye?' Now what had Amos been blurting out?

'I overheard some talk of poison in the fields the other evening and checked with him. He said it wasn't anything important but added that Beckindale had had its dramas. I of course had come to research into two of them – the death of Sharon Crossthwaite, and the more recent attack on Wendy Hotson.'

'I still don't see – ?'

'Sharon Crossthwaite was a relative?'

Annie now understood that Amos had divulged this fact.

She was vexed with him. 'Yes, quite true. The Pearsons and the Crossthwaites are second cousins.'

'Pearson was your maiden name.'

'Yes.'

'It must have grieved you very much, the senseless murder of your young cousin – '

'We were all grieved, Mr Hilleley. This is a close community.'

'Your father, Mr Pearson – visited the bereaved parents? Attended the funeral?'

'Mr Hilleley, it's all a long time ago. As far as relationships are concerned Sharon's mother Beryl was my second or third cousin – not exactly what you'd call family. My father attended the funeral, but so did every man in Beckindale who could get time off.'

'But he must have felt it somewhat more keenly? How did he feel – angry? Vengeful?'

Annie had not invited him to sit. Now she turned her glance towards the door, as if thinking she'd be glad to see him go through it. She said in a tone of dangerous calm: 'Vengeful? "Vengeance is mine, saith the Lord".'

'Your son Jack would hardly subscribe to – orthodox Christian views. Was he very angry? I ask because Latimer, the murderer, is due out on parole soon.'

'I don't think there's any way I can help you, Mr Hilleley,' she said, and went to the door.

Before she could put her hand on the doorknob he said: 'Your son found Wendy Hotson?'

She paused, turned. 'My son Joe – yes.'

'That must have been a dreadful experience for him – '

'Yes.'

'He's left the village, I understand?'

Annie opened the door with a sudden curt movement. 'I don't like the sound of your book, Mr Hilleley. Happen your intentions are right but I wonder what your methods will achieve? If you don't mind, I'll get back to my work.'

'Could it be that there are things in those cases you don't want brought out, Mrs Sugden?' he demanded, coming out into the open.

Annie's face went cold. 'I like to think of myself as a Christian woman who thinks evil of none without cause,' she said. 'But if you're writing a book that's supposed to help people, all I can say is I think they're better off without it.'

'I – '

'I want to hear no more, young man. Out please!'

'You realize that your unwillingness to discuss it makes me think – '

'What you think is of no interest to me. Out!'

Hilleley tried to think of some way to retrieve his mistakes but for once his fertile imagination let him down. In face of her cold disdain, he could only shrug and go out.

She closed the door on him. She felt she needed a bath to get rid of the dirt he had dragged in with him.

As he drove down to the village from the farm, Hilleley kept an eye out for Jack Sugden. He didn't see him, but Judy Westrop came into view round a bend of the road. He slowed and stopped. 'Hello, where are you off to?'

'Up to Emmerdale to see the Sugdens.'

He thought he'd better get his defence in quickly. 'I've just been thrown out of there,' he said. 'Got the wrong side of Mrs Sugden.'

'Of Annie?' She stared at him. 'But how?'

'Oh, I don't know. I was just trying to get some background for my book. She knew the Crossthwaites, the family of the girl who was murdered. I shouldn't have mentioned it, perhaps.'

'Not tactful,' she suggested. 'It's a touchy thing you're doing, Paul. I'll see if I can smooth things over – '

'I'd rather you didn't mention it,' he said hastily. Then added, 'Though if it does come up, could you find out where the Crossthwaite family moved to? They've left the village.'

'If it's important . . .' She sounded dubious.

'What are you going up there for, anyway?'

'There was some talk that I could move into Demdyke while Joe was away.'

'Demdyke?'

'His cottage in Demdyke Row. I need a place to stay for a while. Richard Anstey doesn't exactly make me feel unwelcome at Home Farm but I have the notion he'd be glad to see me go. I'm moving to a flat in Hotten, but it's not ready yet and . . .'

'Listen, shall we meet in the pub tonight? If you've found out where Mr and Mrs Crossthwaite have gone, you can tell me then.'

'Righto.' She stood back, waved as he drove off. She was a little perturbed, but didn't quite know why.

Annie was pleased to see her. At her question about Demdyke, she nodded at once. 'I should think there's no problem over that. Joe's likely to be away until July – he wants to watch harvesting methods in the States. It's silly to have it standing empty.'

'And by then my flat should be ready. All I need now is a good job.'

'I know where there's a good job,' Dolly said, looking up from setting the table for the evening meal.

'Where, Dolly?'

'At Huxley's, the auctioneers. I got details of it for myself.'

'Oh . . . then . . .'

'I've decided not to apply.' She gave a little sidewise smile to Annie. 'I'll do something, I think, but not a full-time job so far off from the farm. Feel free to go after it.'

'Honestly, Dolly?'

'The details are on that sheet there – I got it from the Hotten Bureau in Field Road.'

'That's grand, I'll ring them first thing tomorrow.'

'Why don't you ring now? It's only just gone five. They'll still be there. Ask for an appointment.'

Annie laughed at the enthusiasm the two girls were engendering. She indicated the telephone. 'Go ahead, Judy, strike while the iron's hot.'

When Sam came in for his meal, he found them discussing the best way for Judy to dress for the interview. Women's talk, he muttered to himself, and was glad when Matt and Jack came in so that he could discuss the crops with them. They teased him about being jealous of Amos's allotment but learned they were maligning him when they thought he'd been to look at it.

'I were giving t'vicar a hand in the churchyard. Wanted sorting, that did. And guess who I saw there?' he added, with a glance at his grandson. 'Pat Merrick – tidying up her mother's grave and putting flowers on it.'

Jack made no response. Matt said, 'I noticed it were looking neglected. A bit beyond Elsie Harker to do much, I s'pose. And the rest of the family's gone.'

'Aye, like the Crossthwaites,' Sam said, bringing in the name that Hilleley had enquired about. 'I saw that writer feller looking at their headstones again.'

'Where did the family go?' Judy queried. 'Do you mean they're dead?'

'Nay, Scarborough – Beryl and her husband couldn't abide Beckindale after what happened to Sharon. Somewhere near t'coach park, wasn't it, Annie? Falgrave Terrace, or summat.'

But Annie was busy with checking the food in the oven, and either didn't hear or didn't want to.

Since the meal was nearly ready Judy took her leave, despite invitations to join them. As they ate, Jack related his intentions about the pedigree herd and said he would ring Joe at the camp-site during the night. Sam was indignant. 'The middle of the night? It's not natural,' he protested. ''Sides, you haven't got the phone number.'

'I can get that from directory enquiries, Grandad.'

The old man shook his head. 'I can't see why it's so urgent.'

'I suppose it isn't. I could write. But the letter might miss him. They're moving around a lot – at least I know if I ring tonight, they really are at the Lone Pine Trailer Park.'

'I bet you'll sleep right through and never do it,' Matt teased.

'No, I won't. I'm going to go down to the Woolpack, spend a pleasant hour or so playing darts, go to bed at ten, and be wide awake and eager the minute my alarm rings at four o'clock.'

'Wake me up so I can witness all this,' Matt suggested.

'Don't you dare!' This was Dolly.

Sam couldn't get them to treat it seriously. By the time

the meal ended he wasn't even sure whether it was a joke or not.

But Jack really meant to ring Joe. He went to the Woolpack with Matt and Dolly, one part of his mind taking part in their conversation and the other rehearsing what he'd say to his brother. It would need to be cogently expressed; after all, they would be on a transatlantic line and time was money. But he wanted to be sure that Joe understood his intentions. There was no thought in his mind of trying to take control of the herd away from Joe. All he wanted was to help improve it.

Judy Westrop was there when they arrived, chatting with Hilleley. Dolly said: 'There's that man, still here. You'd think he'd move on to other cases if he's got a whole book to do.'

'The explanation's quite simple, love. He's taken a fancy to Judy.'

Dolly looked in surprise at her husband. 'You know,' she said, 'that never occurred to me. I can see Judy likes him, but . . . I must be wrong, I suppose. I just didn't see him showing any affection for *her*.'

Jack's darts companions had not yet shown up. They settled down with their drinks. There was a fairly large gathering in the bar for the men had several things to discuss – the forthcoming cricket match between Robblesfield and Beckindale, the dates of the various horticultural and craft shows of the summer, and the scheduling of the harvests.

So it was in front of a full house that something happened which had been looked forward to by most of Beckindale. Pat Merrick walked in.

'Oh, heck,' Amos said to Henry. 'She's here.'

'Who?'

'Pat Merrick.'

Hilleley, further along the bar talking to Judy, overheard. He turned to look at Jack Sugden's girl.

She was an attractive enough young woman, wearing a chain store dress and very little make-up. She was nothing like the sex-kittens his name had been linked with in Rome.

'Ah, it was all years ago, Amos,' Henry said. As Pat

reached the bar he said to her, 'Nice to see you in the Woolpack, Pat. What'll it be?'

'Just some cigarettes, please. Twenty king-size if you have them.'

Henry turned to get them. She put the money down to pay for them and as she did so, saw that his gaze was directed beyond her to someone at the far side of the room. She turned.

Jack Sugden was staring straight at her. He half rose from his chair. 'Pat!' he exclaimed.

With a strange intake of breath, she turned and without picking up the cigarettes hurried out of the bar.

Amos shook his head. 'Years don't seem to have made much difference, Mr Wilks,' he remarked, and nodded at Jack Sugden.

Jack was shouldering his way through the crowd to follow her. And Hilleley was observing him with avid interest.

Chapter Eight

It wasn't easy to catch up with Pat. She really intended to evade him. But Jack was determined to speak to her.

She had hurried off without much sense of direction. In a steep lane leading up to The Struggle, she had to pause to catch her breath.

It was twilight. But she recognized the man who approached her. 'Why did you go rushing away like that?' he asked.

She shrugged, unable to explain. It surprised her, almost, that he needed an explanation.

'I thought you'd mebbe get in touch, Pat,' he went on. 'I knew of course you'd come back to the village.'

'I didn't want to spoil your holiday.'

'Holiday?' He gave a little laugh of protest. 'I'm home for good, Pat.'

She peered up at him in the failing light. 'You mean you prefer Beckindale to all that sunshine and glamour?'

'It's not really like that. And after a bit you begin to think that . . . it would be nice to belong somewhere.' He thrust all that aside. 'How's Tom?'

'Same as ever,' she said in a flat voice.

'He's here with you?' When she shook her head with sudden vehemence he went on: 'How about the kids?'

'Oh, they're fine.' She didn't want to discuss them. 'I must be getting back. Auntie will be wondering – '

'Jackie must be . . . what . . . fifteen now?'

'Aye.'

'Still at school, of course.'

'They both are.'

'Have things been tough . . .' He tried for a better word . . . 'Hard, for you?'

'I've survived. Had to.'

'If there's anything I can do . . .'

Surely he must know he was the last man she could or would approach? She edged away from him. 'Jack, please . . . I must get back!'

'I'll walk with you.'

She made the beginning of a shake of the head.

'Afraid of gossip?'

'Oh,' she broke out in exasperation, 'it's all right for you! You always were a summer swallow, able to soar through it! But me . . . I see no point in starting tongues wagging again. I had enough o' that in the past.'

'What can they say they haven't said already? Come on, I'm walking with you. It's getting too dark for a lass to be walking alone. There's been some funny things happened, I hear.'

'Nay, lad – '

'Come on.' He took her arm through his. 'Who's to see us, anyway?'

If he had glanced back, he would have found out. Paul Hilleley was watching them with interest from the bend of the road.

It was late when at last Jack Sugden got home. Matt and Dolly had already gone to bed and so had Grandad, but Annie was giving the room a final tidy. 'I thought you were going to be in bed by now?' she queried as he came in.

'I got side-tracked.'

'Still going to ring Joe?'

'Aye.'

'Give him my love.'

'Aye.'

'Owt wrong?'

'No, nothing much. It's all right, Ma. Off you go to your rest.'

He sat for a long time in the quiet kitchen, listening to the steady tick of the old wall clock and the occasional movement of coals in the Aga. The house itself creaked from time to time.

He didn't go to bed, but stretched out on the sofa to doze. At the appointed hour he woke without difficulty and dialled the number he'd already obtained from directory enquiries. His call went through amazingly quickly. The voice on the other side sounded as if it were in the next room. 'Hold it a minute,' it said, 'he's in a camper the far side – it'll take a while to corral him.'

But in about three minutes Joe came on. 'Who's that? Jack?' he burst out in anxiety. 'What's gone wrong?'

'Nothing, Joe, nothing. Everything's fine. It's just that I wanted to get your opinion on something before I do it.'

'What? What are you going to do?' There was apprehension in Joe's tone.

'I'm thinking of buying a couple of pedigree Friesian cows for the herd. What do you say?'

The silence that followed was so long that Jack thought the call had broken down. 'Joe? Are you still there?'

'Aye, but breathless. Pedigree Friesians?'

'I wondered if you would think it a good idea.'

'It's a great idea. But where's the money to come from?'

'I'll pay.'

'You?'

'Aye, it's a worthwhile investment, I think.'

'Jack, are you feeling all right?'

Jack grinned in the darkness of the farm kitchen. 'As well as I could, considering it's four a.m. here.'

'I know that. That's why I was so scared when I heard there was a call for me. I thought . . . Listen, you daft article, what are you up to?'

'Nowt, Joe, honestly. I was talking with Matt and he said how long it would take to up-grade the herd, and then I thought that if I were to put a bit in the kitty and buy some pedigree stock, it would be a faster result. That's right, isn't it?'

'Of course it's right, but – '

'And you want to up-grade the herd, don't you?'

'I certainly do, but – '

'So do you agree I should buy the stock?'

There was a slight pause. 'Have you talked to Henry about this?'

'No. Should I?'

'You should. He's a shareholder and he's got his head screwed on.'

'He can't be against this, surely?'

'Listen, Jack, it isn't just getting pedigree stock. You have to have safe boundaries so no non-pedigree bulls can wander in and get at them – '

'What, in these days of A.I.D.? How many bulls are there in Beckindale?'

'Enough. And then there's housing them. We'd want to improve our mistle – '

'That could come later. But you're right, Henry has to be asked. I'll do that tomorrow.'

'What did Matt say?'

'Not much. He said it was your decision.'

'Mmm . . .'

'What's wrong, Joe?' But he could guess. Joe was a long way off, trying to read his intentions over a long-distance connection. Joe was asking himself, 'Is this another of his sudden impulses? Will he go back on it in a day or two?'

'When do you want to buy them?'

'Soon as possible.'

'That makes sense.' There was something like longing in Joe's voice. If anyone was going to choose pedigree

Friesians, Joe would have wanted it to be himself. 'Have you spoken to Clifford Longthorn?'

'Not yet. But I'm going to if you agree.'

'Let me think on, Jack. I can't jump to a decision half-way through a steak dinner on the other side of the Atlantic.'

'Oh, I interrupted your supper – I'm sorry – '

'Don't be daft, Jack! I only meant you'd got me unprepared. Let me think. Can I ring back?'

'When?'

'Let me sleep on it. I'll try to get you some time tomorrow.'

'That would be good, Joe. Then I could go to Loudwick Market the following day.'

'Bye!' Joe said. 'You don't intend to let t'grass grow under your clogs. Righto, I'll ring tomorrow.'

'Right then. So long for now, Joe.'

'Hey!'

'What?'

'You'd better put your jacket on. It must be near milking time over there. 'Bye!'

Jack put down the receiver. On the whole he was pleased with the conversation. Making allowances for his brother's astonishment, he felt he'd convinced him he was in earnest. The day after tomorrow, he'd be at the market inspecting pedigree cows.

Deep in thought, he quietly made himself a cup of tea in the thin light of dawn. He was so intent on his conversation with Joe that he'd quite forgotten Pat Merrick.

But Paul Hilleley hadn't forgotten her. A few hours later, when the world of Beckindale was on the move and the children were off to school, Hilleley was parked in his car outside the house where Pat Merrick was staying. He had been there over half an hour. When she came out of the house he got out of his car, timing the action so that he reached the gate as she did.

'Good morning. Mrs Merrick, is it?'

'Yes?' said Pat, pausing in surprise with her hand on the gate.

'My name is Hilleley, Paul Hilleley. I'm a friend of Jack's – Jack Sugden.'

'Oh?' She was looking at him warily.

'I'm doing a literary article about his books – for the review column of my paper. Appreciation of his effect on English writing – that kind of thing. Perhaps you could help me?'

She shook her head. ''Fraid not. I'm not up in that kind of thing.'

'Oh, forgive me, I should have explained.' He turned on the charm. 'I'm not asking your critical opinion. I just want a bit of background information. "Village Boy Makes Good" – that kind of thing. You knew him as a lad?'

'Oh, aye – '

'Have you read his books?'

'Only the famous one – *Field of Tares*.'

'Enjoyed it, did you?'

'Yes. But I don't know much about books – '

'You enjoyed it. That's interesting. Felt it was true to life?'

'I suppose so . . . I've never been to London,' she faltered. She had begun to feel quite frightened of this man, despite his good looks and winning manner.

'But I mean as to the character – the man the story's about. You saw Jack in that, did you? That was the boy you grew up with?'

'I thought he . . . Yes . . . It was like him.'

'In the book he's a bit free with the ladies, isn't he?'

Now she was sure she didn't like him. 'Jack could discuss all this better than me.'

'But you know him very well, don't you? He tells me you were great friends at one time before you . . . got married.'

Pat stiffened. 'I really don't want to say any more,' she said, opening the gate and marching past him.

'I was with him in the Woolpack last night, Mrs Merrick, when you ran away from him.'

She paused.

'He was very upset at the time, but he tells me you . . . made it up?'

'Goodbye, Mr Hilleley,' Pat said, and walked away as

fast as she could towards the bus stop for the Hotten bus.

Hilleley eyed her. He could follow and talk to her until the bus came. She could hardly escape him without missing the bus.

But he should have read the local timetable. People in Beckindale didn't come out and hang about unnecessarily. The bus came round the corner as he was debating what to do, and Pat Merrick stepped aboard and was wafted away.

Still, he'd got a lot from their encounter. There was still emotion between those two. He rather wished he'd walked after them last night to see whether Jack went into the house with her, but he hadn't felt like hoofing it and to go back for his car at the Woolpack was difficult. Besides, he'd abandoned Judy Westrop to hurry after Jack and Pat. He didn't want to explain himself to her. So he'd driven back to the Feathers and gone to bed.

This morning he'd looked at the pictures he'd taken from time to time during his stay. He had several of Jack going about his business, several of Pat, and one particularly good one of Pat meeting her children coming out of school in Hotten. The boy, Jackie, was speaking with animation, one arm flung out. The resemblance to Jack Sugden was there if you looked for it – same dark hair and eyes, same square chin, same rather bony physique.

Pleased with himself, Hilleley set off for Scarborough. He didn't even bother to ring Judy Westrop to explain his behaviour. Her usefulness to him was over.

At that time Amos Brearly was vacuuming the floor of the bar-room. His phone rang, and with a tut-tut of annoyance he switched off and went to answer it.

It was the editor of the *Hotten Courier*. 'Is that you, Brearly? Listen, have you had a fellow hanging around the village recently, name of Hilleley?'

'Oh yes, Mr Taylor, I've been on to that. An author doing research about murder and that, for a non-fiction book. I've been doing a piece for the *Courier* about him but it's not as urgent as the bowls match – '

'Author my foot!' cried Taylor. 'He's a scandalmonger

from the *Sunday Gazette*! One of my contacts in Fleet Street tipped me the wink – he's been snooping after something juicy and I want it understood, Brearly – the *Courier* gives him no assistance!'

'Scandalmonger?' Amos gasped.

'The *Courier* doesn't go in for that kind of thing. It will offend our readers if we're in any way connected with it. Understood?'

'Oh aye, Mr Taylor. Aye, I understand . . .' Only too well. Amos was recalling how Paul Hilleley had hurried out after Jack Sugden and Pat Merrick last night. He recalled his own unguarded remarks. He recalled many a little chat he'd had with Hilleley, under the impression that he, Amos, was gathering material for a little piece for the *Courier*: Book Author Investigates Beckindalian Drama for Forthcoming Documentary Volume. It seemed only too likely that Hilleley had been getting information instead of giving it.

'So if he comes pushing his nose into things, you'll tell him nothing. Right?'

'Right, Mr Taylor.'

Oh yes, from now on – nothing! But it was too late, although he didn't know it. Hilleley wouldn't be coming back to the Woolpack.

Judy Westrop came in on her way home from her interview in Hotten. 'I've got the job,' she announced with pride. 'I'm to start next week.'

'That's really great,' Henry said. 'But I expected it.'

'You did?'

'Of course – why not? You're a very intelligent young woman, anyone can see that.'

'Not so intelligent,' she returned with a little frown. 'I got stood up last night – did you notice? Paul went rushing out and never came back.'

'Er . . .' said Amos.

'I thought he might be here now – he often comes in at lunch-time.'

'Er . . .' Amos said again.

'I saw him driving towards Harrogate,' Henry told her. 'I was on my way to Emmerdale for a bit of a conference that

Jack wanted, and Hilleley drove past. Didn't even bother to wave to me.'

'Er . . .' Amos said, with more force. 'If I may get a word in edgeways . . .'

'The only word you've said so far is "er",' Henry said. 'But by all means.'

'My editor rang a while ago. To warn me about Mr Hilleley.'

'Warn you?' Henry looked at Amos. His partner got things wrong so often that it was almost certainly a mistake. All the same, he felt a prickle of foreboding.

'He told me that Hilleley isn't a book writer at all. He's a reporter for the *Sunday Gazette*.'

Aghast, the other two stared at him.

'That rag?' Henry groaned at last.

'But he . . . he told me he . . .' Judy faltered into silence.

'He's been acting a lie!' Amos announced in a tone of doom. 'Worming his way into our confidence and taking advantage of our trust.'

'But, look here, Amos, you always said you thought there was something phoney about him – '

'I did, it's true, but I put it down to the poetic licence – that means a writer can say what he likes without it actually being a lie, you know.'

'Amos!' Henry said. 'Last night . . . !'

'Aye,' Amos agreed.

'What?' Judy asked. 'What are you talking about?'

'He dashed out after Jack and Pat Merrick. You wouldn't know, but there's an old yarn hereabouts concerning Jack and Pat . . .Oh, *lord*,' groaned Henry.

After a long moment Judy sighed. 'That accounts for why he didn't bother to come back,' she said. 'And why he hasn't got in touch to apologize for leaving me high and dry. What a fool I've been!'

'We all have,' Henry said. 'I'm afraid we all have.'

At Emmerdale the phone rang as they were finishing their midday meal. Jack looked at the clock. It was six a.m. in Dakota. When Jack picked up the receiver, it was the voice he expected.

'Did you speak to Henry?' Joe enquired.

'Yes. And he's in favour if you are.'

'He's thought about the additional expense in improving the herd at a greater rate than we foresaw?'

'Yes, but he thinks it's worth it. But only subject to your approval.'

'Aye,' said Joe. 'Well – all right.'

'All right?'

'Got cloth ears? All right. Go ahead.'

'Joe! I'm right glad to hear you say it!'

'I hope we're all going to be glad when we have to cope with the results. We're going to need better calving accommodation, for a start. Can't take the slightest risk with a pedigree calf. Never mind, it's worth it. How's Ma feel about it?'

'You'd better speak to her yourself.' Jack handed over the receiver, guiltily aware that last night he'd passed on none of the messages he'd been given. The rest of the phone call was taken up with the family having a word in turn. Jack went on again at the end, to emphasize that he was going to talk it over with Clifford Longthorn, the breeder of pedigree Friesians, before he made any purchase; also that Matt was going to hold his hand.

As soon as the connection was broken, Jack went out to drive to Longthorn's place, for an educational conversation about Friesians.

Richard Anstey of N.Y. Estates was there when he pulled into the Longthorns' yard. 'Hello, there,' he said to Jack. 'I'm just telling Clifford, I've narrowed down the possibilities about that Enidrin. It must be either Peter Finbar or Ernie Tolly – and my money's on Tolly because he's the type who'd hang on to old stocks of chemicals long after everybody else would dispose of them.'

'Is there any real evidence?'

'None that I know of.'

'So there's no real way of stopping him, whoever it is? He ought to be prosecuted!'

Anstey looked at him with an enquiring expression.

'You're taking it to heart a bit, aren't you? I thought it was us farmers who worried about things like that.'

'I'm a farmer,' Jack protested.

'Thought you were a writer?' Anstey teased.

'Well, I'm an amateur cricketer and a tea-drinker and a baptized member of the Church of England. A man is more than just one thing, you know.'

'And at the moment you're a conservationist.'

'I've always been that. It's just become more important, that's all. Is anything being done to stop Tolly, if that's who it is?'

'I'm going to throw a scare into him. He's a tenant of N.Y. Estates, and I'll tell him if he doesn't hand in all those out of date pesticides to the vet for disposal, we'll take him to court. He'll co-operate. I'll see he does.'

'Threats, Mr Anstey?'

'What would you prefer, Mr Sugden? Dead birds and foxes?'

'No, I'd rather have Tolly scared.'

'Leave it to me,' Anstey said grimly. He shook hands and prepared to leave. 'I'll see what you're offering at market tomorrow,' he said to Longthorn. To Jack he added: 'By the way, you don't know if Judy Westrop has a job yet, do you? Because the girl who runs the playgroup for the N.Y. employees' children is leaving to have a baby, and it's not the sort of thing that I can run myself. So, if you hear of anyone looking for a job locally, I'd be glad to know.'

'It's just an idea,' said Jack, 'but you might ask Dolly. She loves children, and at the moment she needs something to occupy her . . .'

Anstey smiled. 'That's a really good idea. I'll give her a ring and ask her. Thanks a lot. Well, goodbye for the moment.'

'He going to be buying cows tomorrow?' Jack enquired as Anstey drove off.

'Couldn't say. What makes you ask?'

'Well, the thing is,' Jack replied rather nervously, 'I'm in need of a bit of advice about Friesians . . .'

Judy Westrop's pleasure in having landed her job was

marred by the news that Paul Hilleley was a reporter. All afternoon she was plagued by it, so that around seven o'clock she couldn't bear it any longer. She drove to Connelton, to enquire at the reception desk if Mr Hilleley was in the hotel.

'I believe he's in the bar, miss,' the reception clerk told her.

Judy walked in. The bar was rather a pretentious place with lots of horse brasses and hunting prints, but agreeable. Hilleley was sitting at the counter reading a paper and sipping a whisky.

'Hello, Paul,' she said, taking him by surprise by sitting on the stool next to him.

He was startled, but recovered at once. 'Hello, Judy. Fancy seeing you here. Like a drink?'

'You know I don't.'

'Have one of your orange juice specials then.'

'No, thank you. I've come to ask you one question. Why did you rush out after Jack Sugden last night?'

'Did I? I don't remember that.'

'You never told me you were a journalist from the *Sunday Gazette*.'

'Oh.' He picked up his glass, looked at the whisky through the light, then sipped. 'Well, that was my business.'

'Your business is to rake up muck, I take it. Have you finished in Beckindale?'

'Yes, I think I have. Only a little interview to do in Bradford tomorrow, then to London to do my piece. But I'll be back in Connelton in time to see how the news hits the Dales.'

'Bradford?'

'That's where Pat Merrick's husband lives.'

'You're not going to interview her husband!'

'I certainly am. "Deserted Husband Accuses Sugden" – that's a real pippin.'

Judy studied him with disbelief. 'You're detestable,' she murmured.

'Depends how you look at me. My editor thinks I'm the tops.'

'I hope I never see or hear of you again!'

'Oh, you'll hear of me, girlie. Buy the *Sunday Gazette* next Sunday. I'm going to give Beckindale something to gossip about!'

She turned on her heel, and walked out.

Chapter Nine

The newspapers were delivered to the village shop on a Sunday by a van which came from a warehouse in Leeds. The driver had no particular interest in the contents of the papers or the villages he passed through. It was his aim to have them on the doorsteps outside the shops by seven in the morning so that he could be back home in time for breakfast. Then off out fishing – that was his sole thought.

Mrs Shore opened the shop at eight, sorted out the papers, and had everything ready for her first customers at eight-thirty.

Amos Brearly was one of her first customers. He always bought the Sunday version of his daily paper. Behind him came Seth Armstrong with his pointer at his heels. He bought a copy of the *Gazette*.

At nine o'clock the boy who made the deliveries arrived, loaded up the basket on his bike, and cycled off. He passed Seth Armstrong leaning against a low wall in the morning sunshine, reading his paper with an expression of mingled horror and amazement.

One of the first houses he visited was Mrs Harker at Drygrounds. There he left one of the northern cosy weeklies, and a copy of the *Gazette*. He circled round and put the newspapers through letterboxes or in containers at farm gates. He was back in Beckindale by nine-thirty.

Jack Sugden was upstairs by that time, getting changed after having finished milking. He came down about ten, looking neat and spruce in a suit and tie.

'Coming to church, then?' his mother asked with a smile.

'Aye, I thought I'd give thanks to the Lord for not making any mistakes in buying those Friesians. Worst day of my life, that was – I was shaking with nerves. But when I read out their pedigrees on the phone to Joe, he sounded quite chuffed.'

'At them prices, they ought to give gold top milk in gold bottles,' muttered Sam. Pleased though he was at the idea of Emmerdale having a pedigree herd, he was nevertheless put out at the thought of all that money.

The phone rang. Jack was nearest, and answered it.

To his astonishment, it was Pat Merrick. 'Jack? Is that you? Oh, thank goodness it was you that answered. Jack, have you seen the *Sunday Gazette*?'

'Nay, lass, we don't get that here – '

'Jack, it's awful. Your name and mine are plastered all over it.'

'How d'you mean?'

'It's . . . that feller Hilleley . . . he's made everything sound so . . . I don't know how he could do it! Jack, Auntie Elsie is beside herself – and it's made me feel . . .'

'Leave it with me, lass. I'll handle it.' He put down the phone and looked round at his family, who were watching him in some concern. 'I'll mebbe be a bit late for church. I've a bit of business to attend to.'

He stalked out, white with anger. His grandfather said: 'Business? On the Sabbath?'

'I think that was Pat Merrick on the phone,' Dolly said. 'I thought I just caught . . .'

'I hope he's not going to see that girl,' Sam objected in a tone of reproof. 'We don't want *that* starting all over again!'

Jack had driven off in the Land-Rover at a fast pace. He saw the delivery boy in the High Street and bought a copy of the *Gazette* from him.

A flying headline on the front page announced: 'Jet-set Author's Secret Life: Our Special Feature, Page Eighteen'. He turned to the centre spread. There was his photograph, coming out of the Woolpack with Old Walter and carrying two bottles of Monks Ale – they belonged to Walter but no one would have guessed that. 'Rustic Revelry,' said the caption. Under a photograph of Pat meeting Jackie from the comprehensive the caption ran: 'His Past and His Future?'

He read the text. It was an extraordinary blend of fact and innuendo, which nudged the reader to think it odd how the Sugden men kept being connected with dramas in which girls figured. Pat's return to Beckindale at the same time as Jack came home was pointed out. An interview with Pat's husband was featured in a special box: 'Deserted Husband Speaks: Hasn't He Done Enough To Me?' The effect was to leave the reader with the impression that Beckindale seethed with physical passion, that the Sugdens were always in the thick of it, and that most of the village families wouldn't trust their womenfolk anywhere near the Sugdens.

Old Nellie Ratcliffe had her copy of the *Gazette* ready to read with her second pot of tea. When she saw what was in the centre spread she folded it hastily, pulled on her coat and hat, and hurried out. Nellie was an old friend of the Sugdens, had even once been on the point of marrying Sam Pearson. She went as fast as she could up the High Street and Vicarage Lane. The vicar was just coming out of his gate, on his way to make sure the church was ready for morning service.

'Vicar, vicar! Have you seen this?' She thrust the paper at him.

Mr Hinton eyed it. 'No, Mrs Ratcliffe, I don't read that one.'

'Read it now, vicar! Quick, before the congregation gets gathered. For you'll have something to do and say about this, I'll be bound. And if you haven't, then I'll never set foot in church again!'

'Threats, Mrs Ratcliffe?' Hinton said in good humour, and opened the paper. But the smile died from his face as he read.

'Well, Mr Hinton?'

'There's only one word for this, Mrs Ratcliffe. It's evil.'

'Aye,' she said. She turned away. 'Well, I'll go back home and get myself a bit tidier for service. Think on, vicar.'

By ten-fifteen some of the congregation had gone into the church. Others were gathered in groups outside, talking in hushed, shocked voices. They broke off as the party from Emmerdale walked through the churchyard.

They made their way to the Sugden pew. All of them were aware of heads turning as they did so.

Annie was in the habit of closing her eyes and making herself quiet for a minute or two before church service. When she opened her eyes this morning, she found Alice Dowland leaning over her. 'Annie,' she whispered, 'it's only decent to let you know about this, since I can see you're in the dark.' She passed over a folded newspaper.

Annie opened it. She read, her face going first red and then white. She passed it to Matt, who shared it with Dolly as they read. Sam, disapproving, was about to refuse to take it, but Matt said quietly, 'Read it, Grandad.' Sam did so.

He was about to jump up in anger when there was a stir and the choir came in.

The service began. If the voices were a little unsteady at first, they settled down after the first verse. The vicar led them through the familiar service until at last the time came for him to mount the pulpit.

His sermon, prepared with much thought during the preceding week, lay in a couple of folded sheets on the ledge of the pulpit. He picked it up, opened it out, then after a moment's hesitation put it away. He retraced his steps, went to Peter Barnton in the front row, and took from the ledge beside the prayer book a copy of the *Gazette*. Then he went back up the pulpit steps while the villagers stared at him in astonishment.

He held up the newspaper. 'I don't suppose many of you read this. It has an unsavoury reputation, and deserves it.' He looked out at the congregation, then threw the paper down inside the pulpit. 'But we are only human and today we have read it because it contains something that concerns us all. I should like to deal first with a serious implication concerning the death eight years ago of Sharon Crossthwaite. I was not your priest then but I have heard all about it. It grieved and shocked the village, the more so as a young member of the community confessed to the crime.'

There was a rustling among the listeners.

'In this newspaper article there seems a suggestion that more was known than came out. There is also a suggestion that some people here harbour feelings of revenge against the murderer.'

A faint murmur could be heard. Hinton was too experienced to think that everyone in Beckindale would welcome Jim Latimer if he came home. But he went on in a strong, steadfast tone: 'We judge the world around us by our own experience. If we expect forgiveness, we must extend forgiveness. And to men who could write the kind of nonsense contained in this article, we must extend forgiveness also. Fortunately most journalists are responsible people concerned with truth, who would condemn scandal and innuendo as readily as we do, but a free press is an essential part of our civilization, and even this contemptible example of freedom – more properly licence – may serve to remind us that hasty judgements and easy conclusions are always suspect. My friends, we have all looked about us and thought, "He is behaving wrongly" or "She has no respect for principles". We condemn before we consider. If after reading this newspaper you are tempted to make any kind of judgement on the behaviour of your fellow men, I beg you to remember that sacred admonition: Let him that is without sin among you cast the first stone.'

He paused. He had felt it his duty to deal with the newspaper article but he didn't want to trespass into the private affairs of any of his parishioners. He had gone far enough, he felt.

'This has been a short sermon, and not the one I prepared. Whether it deals adequately with this shock to our community I cannot tell, but it is heartfelt in its appeal.'

He looked at the hymn-board. 'I know our choir is not prepared but I know our organist will lead them now in Hymn Number 269, Who Is On the Lord's Side?'

The congregation rose. The organist, taken by surprise, shuffled through her music. The choir looked at each other. The chord of G major rang out.

With one voice the people began to sing.

Jack Sugden, unaware that the vicar of Beckindale had more or less preached a sermon about him, drove into Connelton. He parked outside the Feathers. At the reception desk he was told that Mr Hilleley had not yet left the hotel although he had asked for his bill to be ready after lunch. 'I think he's out in the garden, reading the papers,' the clerk suggested.

'Thank you,' said Jack. True enough, he found the journalist at the far side of the lawn, beside a pretty oval pond on which a pair of mallards were swimming. 'Morning, Hilleley,' Jack said.

'Oh! Morning, Sugden.'

'I've been reading a bit of your work here,' Jack went on, holding out the folded newspaper.

'You have? Didn't like it much, eh? But don't get on your high horse. It's all properly researched – nothing libellous, I had the law men look through it.'

'Aye, you're very careful over that. You don't exactly say that I'm waiting with a cudgel for Jim Latimer, but it's implied.'

'The girl he murdered was related to you, after all.'

'About ten times removed. You didn't mention that.'

'There's only room for so much information, old boy. Can't tell the reader every little thing.' Hilleley shrugged and threw a scrap of bread to the ducks.

'But there was room to drag in the fact that I'm very friendly with a married woman who lives here. There was room to report the views of her husband. You're very selective in what you print.'

'It's a human interest story. Come on, Sugden, don't kid yourself. You know you have to pay for being in the public eye, and it does help the sales of your books, now doesn't it?'

'I don't need that kind of help,' Jack said, moving a step nearer.

Hilleley eyed him. 'What are you going to do about it? Sue me? All that will do is to build it up even more. And you'd lose anyhow. I made sure there was nothing actionable – or at least my editor did.' He chuckled. 'Chirman knows what he's about. As he says, in the end you'll be glad of the free publicity.'

'I don't want publicity at the expense of innocent people. I came home to get away from all that. Now you've pulled your muckrake over everything – '

'Oh, spoiled your country idyll, did I? Don't be an innocent, man! Everybody knew all about your floozie – '

Jack seized him by the lapels of his suede jacket. 'I don't believe in violence but by God there are times I understand how folk are driven to it!'

'Let go of me!' the other man gasped, fright contorting his features so that the superior expression was gone.

'You're not worth being violent with,' Jack said, pulling away from him. The impulse of anger had gone, leaving only disgust. 'You're dirt . . . muck . . . you're slimy . . . and the best thing I can do with you is send you back where you belong!'

He gave him a shove. Hilleley went backwards into the duckpond. He went under. The ducks took off in a clatter of wings and flailing feet, to circle the hotel. Hilleley disappeared under the water and came up again, gasping and thrashing. Green weeds and algae draped over him, head and shoulders. Gasping for breath, he staggered towards the edge. Jack waited until he was within a foot or two then held out his hand. Hilleley took it.

Jack pulled. At the same time he put out a foot and shoved. Hilleley's legs went from under him. Jack let go his hand. Down went the reporter, face first. He made frantic swimming motions but the water was only four feet deep. In a moment he found bottom and stood up again.

Jack looked at him and nodded. 'I hope your editor will pay for cleaning your jacket,' he remarked, turned on his heel, and strode away.

As he re-entered the hotel a waiter was hurrying towards the lawn, attracted by Hilleley's outcry. 'What's the matter, sir?' he asked.

'One of your guests has taken a very necessary bath, but I don't think he's clean yet,' Jack replied. 'Good morning.'

He got into the Land-Rover and drove away without further check. Honour was satisfied; he had made Hilleley pay for what he had written.

But the damage was done, and nothing could undo it.

Chapter Ten

Joe returned home towards the end of July, having stayed long enough to see the beginning of both the wheat and corn harvest. He brought gifts for everyone and lots of enthusiasm for American know-how.

'Of course over there everything is on a huge scale. And the machinery matches it. I'm not saying it would do here, not at all. But it's not just the size of the machines. It's the way they think everything through. They analyse their weather prospects and have their machines lined up ready to go on the day the crop will be ready. They have back-up services for the machinery. If owt goes wrong, they have spare parts – '

'Takes a lot of brass, all that,' Matt supposed.

'Oh aye. They *invest*. Farming's big business out there. Though I must say, Ed is spending money as if it were water on that farm of his – I think he's beginning to realize farming's not a cheap game with easy rewards. Still the Americans really plough money back into their land . . .'

'Like N.Y. Estates.'

'Bigger.'

'Well, we've invested,' Jack remarked. 'We've got ourselves the beginnings of a pedigree herd.'

'Aye, and right tidy beasts they are too, Jack. You did well there.'

Jack smiled to himself at this accolade from his brother. It pleased him but it amused him. Joe was taking it for granted that until he said it was a good purchase, Jack's action had been in doubt.

'And what we want now,' Joe went on, 'is the follow-through. We've got to keep it all up to scratch, and more – we've got to better it. There's other things besides cows that this farm should pay attention to.'

'You mean you think I could have made better use of my money?'

'You couldn't have got better cows. I approve o' them in every way. But I reckon a new Land-Rover would hav done the farm more good than a couple of pedigre Friesians.'

Jack opened his mouth to object. Joe went on quickly 'Nay, nay, I'm not griping about buying 'em. I'm only sayin that if I'd been here and we'd talked it through properly happen you'd have seen what needed buying most.'

Jack looked at Matt. 'Is that your view?'

'It's a fact our Land-Rover has seen better days,' Mat said thoughtfully.

'You never said that on the phone when we talked,' Jack pointed out, with a wry glance at Joe.

'Well, no . . . I can get carried away too, especially at tha distance. It's not a way to do business, Jack – all of a sudden without prior notification, making up your mind abou buying cows. I thought it over for a few hours and the conclusion I came to was that if I said we needed a new Land-Rover more, you wouldn't buy a Land-Rover. But if I said we could build up a herd with pedigree cows, you'd buy cows. Am I right?'

There was a silence. Then Jack smiled and shrugged. 'Right,' he said.

Matt looked from one brother to the other. If Joe was hoping that Jack would now say, 'Let's buy a Land-Rover too,' he was going to be disappointed. For the moment Jack had taken enough action. He had an interest in the herd, and wanted to learn more about it. Perhaps he didn't have any more money to invest. No one knew what his financial situation was. He didn't talk about such things.

Later in the morning Matt went over to Partlett's Farm to help with their barley harvest. There he found Henry pitching in.

'How's Joe settling in?' Henry asked, pausing to wipe sweat from his brow as he helped heave baled straw.

'Not bad. He and Jack keep having a long discussion – '

'Joe wants to go into machinery, does he? I expected that – '

'Nay, he's learned the opposite – that machinery only

pays its use on really big stretches. Nay, it's a bit more fundamental, in a way. Joe is pointing out that Jack's view of farming is different from his. Jack wants to concentrate on the livestock, the natural things. Joe says – and he's got a point – that we'd have been better off with a new Land-Rover.'

'Does he, now.' Henry was called to go back to his place in the line of workmen, and left with a nod. But he thought about Matt's words. Joe was right. However delightful it was to have the beginnings of a pedigree herd, it would have been more to the point to get their premises ready for them first, to have transport available for their offspring when they came, and better calving pens.

And yet . . . Perhaps Jack with his small-scale view of farming would prove to be in the right. Emmerdale could never do things on a big scale unless it merged with a business like N.Y. Estates. Joe, bright and ambitious, was never going to do better than run Emmerdale efficiently on the scale to which it would work. Jack would be content with that; perhaps Joe would not.

Richard Anstey was interested to hear what Joe had felt about his visit to the States. 'Did you visit any of their seed testing stations? They do massive research into new strains of seed, I remember.'

'No, Ed hadn't arranged any visits. I had to rely on him, you know, Richard.'

'I didn't really know Ed Hathersage. What kind of a farm is he buying?'

'Oh, you should see it! It's a model wheat-producing place. I tried once or twice to hint to him that the cost of keeping it up to that standard was going to be high, especially with his government putting embargoes on exports of wheat to the Soviets. But Ed's a bit of a dreamer, in a way. He's got a kind of a seven-year-itch – wants to start all over again and do it better.'

'I know the feeling,' Anstey laughed. He rose to fetch the whisky bottle. 'Top you up?'

'No thanks, Richard – I've got to drive back.'

'Ever thought of starting again yourself?'

Joe laughed and leaned back in the buttoned leather armchair, stretching out his legs. 'Have I not! New start, new place – money to do it *my* way . . .'

'Your way?'

'Well, see, I'm trapped in my inheritance, aren't I? Emmerdale is a hill farm, formed by generations of hill farmers and limited by the climate and soil. No way to do much with it unless I had funds. But I've seen things now that make me realize my horizons have been closed off. I'd like to learn . . . Wish now I'd been a bit of a scholar and gone to agricultural college.'

Anstey shook his dark head, sipped his whisky, and looked thoughtful. 'I went to agricultural college. When I started in farm management, I realized I'd learned nothing. Oh, I knew how to test soil and recognize disease and measure milk yields against records and work out which crops I ought to try for the best results. But I learnt nothing about how to manage men, how to work into a community. That took me five more years.'

They said no more for a moment. Then Anstey took up the word again. 'That playgroup of ours, for the children of our workers. When I left college, nobody told me I'd have to find staff to run things like that.'

'It was good of you to let our Dolly have the chance of a job there,' Joe acknowledged. 'She's loving it.'

'She's ideal for the job. But that's the point, Joe – what do you do when you can't find ideal people?'

'Make do with second best.'

'And then you have to watch your staff all the time – it gets very tiring!'

'Aye, I suppose so.'

Anstey eyed him over his tumbler. 'Ever thought of leaving Emmerdale Farm, Joe?'

'You what?'

'Leaving it. Going somewhere else.'

'Where, for instance? America?' Joe shook his head. 'Ed offered me a job. It's out of the question. Who'd run Emmerdale?'

'That would be a problem, I suppose.'

'You bet,' said Joe.

They finished their drinks and went out to dinner together. Anstey said no more about change. He was satisfied with what he'd achieved so far.

Joe moved back into Demdyke, Judy Westrop having moved to her flat in Hotten. It was Judy who alerted them to another slight shake-up – she had heard it through her work with the auctioneer, Huxley.

'Is that right Ed Hathersage may have to sell the land he donated for the Farm Museum?' she asked.

'You haven't been told it's back on the market?' Joe countered.

'No, but there's a bit of looking at old inventories and so forth. Is it on the cards?'

'I don't think he can alter the legal documents he signed when he handed it over to the county. But I sort of think he regrets it now,' Joe admitted. 'He's finding it expensive, working that place of his in Dakota.'

'It'd be an awful blow to Geoff Atwill – '

'The whole thing was over-optimistic, if you ask me,' Joe remarked. 'I was glad of it at the time because we got sixty acres we badly needed. But I could never see how Geoff could make the place run smoothly on a part-time basis. And now look what's happened – he's been sent on a job to Scotland, and the experts he thought would help him haven't turned up.'

Joe's grandfather was upset by the whole thing. 'There's weeds growing in them fields,' he moaned. 'Weeds! And the old machinery isn't being properly looked after – it'll rust, tha knows, if it's not kept oiled. And when I think of all the work I put into that martingale for the horses – and where are the horses, I'd like to know? Not one has been bought.'

'Just as well,' Jack pointed out. 'There's nobody there to look after them.'

'Huh!' said Sam in high dudgeon, and stamped out. He wasn't pleased with life at the moment. He was watching Jack like a hawk, prepared to lecture him if he spent any time with Pat Merrick and disappointed that, in fact, Jack seemed never to exchange a single word with her. Although

Beckindale had taken the vicar's sermon to heart, it had affected them. Sam's cronies couldn't resist an occasional dig at him about his glamorous grandsons, one of them famous in the newspapers and the other a whizzkid who rushed off to America.

He had an appointment with Seth Armstrong at the church hall. What it was for, he couldn't imagine. Seth was the moving spirit in the Beckindale Allotments Association and did most of the work arranging the Horticultural Show, so Sam suspected he was about to be conned in some way – persuaded not to enter some of his produce so that Seth could get first prize. But he wasn't going to fall for that.

The church hall was in use today for a meeting of the dog-training society. Strictly speaking, Seth and Sam had no right to be there, since they didn't take their dogs along. But there was tea to be had when the church hall was in use. They bought themselves two cups and sat down on hard, rather dusty chairs.

Sam couldn't get the hang of what Seth was after. He seemed to want to give Sam advice about the annual cricket match between Beckindale and Robblesfield.

'I hear it's to be a Saturday this year, Sam,' he remarked. 'What's t'point of that? Early closing day's Thursday – '

'Them as plays don't have early closing days,' Sam said. 'And we'd get nobody watching if we played any other day than Saturday.'

'But you've hopped it forward a week this year, Sam.'

Sam tapped his nose. 'Our fast bowler'll be in Majorca the following Saturday.'

'Oh, I see. But if you had it on a Thursday – ?'

'Thursday – what'd be the point of that?'

'Robblesfield's leg spinner, Bob Edgeley – he couldn't turn up on a Thursday 'cos he goes to Loudwick Market that day – '

'What you on about, Seth? I've fixed the date and that's that.'

A look of desperation flashed over Seth's narrow features. 'It's the same day as the Horticultural Show!'

Sam let this news sink in. Then he said, with dignity, 'Then you'll have to change the date, lad.'

'Me change? Nowt o' t'sort! You'll have to – '

'The date of the Robblesfield game were fixed ages ago. You should have consulted – '

'I don't settle the date,' Seth intervened. 'It's the committee.'

'Lot o' spineless gumps who do as you tell 'em! You know as well as I do, Seth – you chose that date. You'll have to choose again.'

'I will not! The Horticultural Show is more important than that daft match with Robblesfield.'

'The Robblesfield match is a matter of honour wi' the whole village, Seth Armstrong. If you've dug yourself a pit and made it impossible for half the men to enter the Flower Show, that's your funeral. And funeral it'll be when they hear! You'd best get back to your *committee* and tell 'em it's all been changed.'

'I'll do no such thing, Sam Pearson! And let me tell you this – you can dose that marrow o' yours with sugar-water till you're blue in the face, but I'm entering one as'll make it look like a banana!'

'Ssh,' said the dog handlers, looking round from their lecture.

Seth got up and strode to the door. Sam waved to him. 'Buy a calendar,' he called.

To console himself Seth went to his allotment. There, hidden from envious eyes on a mound behind his toolshed, was the pride of his life: a monstrous marrow, carefully nurtured to be at its best for the show.

What was the point of it all? he asked himself in despair. Why was he growing this prize marrow, if no one was going to the Show? His triumph would be minimal if the rest of Beckindale was elsewhere.

He stooped to look at it under its cloak of leaves. Dear, plump thing . . . *Full many a flower is born to blush unseen*, as the poet said.

Amos Brearly was gardening today. He advanced upon his plot with a weary tread, for truth to tell it wasn't turning out as well as he'd been led to expect by Dr Torrance's book.

Seth Armstrong was stooping behind his shed, applying some potion from a bottle to a pile of leaves – or so it seemed. Amos paused to watch. Seth, aware of the hairs on the back of his neck prickling, glanced round.

'What d'you want, Amos Brearly?'

'Nowt,' Amos replied. 'Just watching out of horticultural interest.'

'It'd pay you to take an interest in your own plot,' Seth said cuttingly. 'It's a right mess.'

'It is not. There's more in it than meets the eye.'

'You mean wasted seeds and stunted seedlings, I s'pose. Sitha, Amos, you can't have weeds and crops.'

'I . . . er . . . do feel perhaps the weeds want managing a bit. But I haven't got a hoe.'

Seth wanted above all to get rid of Amos. He wanted no one to see his prize product. 'I'll lend you mine,' he said, and fetched it from his shed. 'Get them weeds under control,' he ordered. 'I get 'em spreading to my patch – and I don't agree with your daft ideas about letting weeds get the upper hand.'

Amos nodded towards the object Seth had been tending. 'That don't seem to have suffered.'

Seth leaned towards him. 'Say nowt to Sam Pearson about seeing that marrow, Amos. I'm going to beat him into the ground at the Show.' Pride overcame him. He parted the big leaves and let Amos have a view.

'Oh,' said Amos, impressed. 'You think that'll win?'

'I do.'

'Sam Pearson's a hard man to beat when it comes to veg.'

'Ah!' Seth took from his pocket a bottle containing some dark liquid, and shook it. 'Sam hasn't got the Armstrong secret formula for vegetable marrows! He doesn't stand a chance.'

'Er . . . Seth . . . I couldn't help noticing, on my notice-board – the date of the Flower Show's the same as the cricket match – '

'Don't thee worry about that, lad,' Seth said. 'I'm bending my great mind to it. I'll get Sam Pearson to change his date, see if I don't.'

Amos shrugged and moved away. When he reached his own plot he couldn't help feeling that it really didn't look as good as Seth's. Happen the weeds were a bit overgrown. He took hold of the hoe and began to have a hack at them.

Amos had little idea how to handle a hoe. He therefore went about it gingerly, and in a moment the tool came up against something solid.

A stone? But he'd cleared all stones from his plot before he made his deep bed. Besides, this was softer than a stone. He knelt to examine what he had touched. It was masked by large, plate-like leaves with rather hairy surfaces. He parted the leaves.

There, reclining like a barrage balloon, was the largest vegetable marrow Amos had ever seen.

He felt a pang of protective love. It was his! He had grown it! And it was big enough to win a prize over even Seth Armstrong and Sam Pearson. Hastily he covered it up again. No one must know. He would produce it on the day of the Show, to everyone's amazement, and walk off with first prize in the marrow section.

The days went by. Seth tried by various dirty-trick tactics to get Sam to alter the date of the cricket match. Sam refused to be intimidated. And then the powers that be, deciding it was time for Seth to have his come-uppance, struck. They chose the shape of Richard Anstey for this moment.

'By the way,' Anstey said to his gamekeeper after a short discussion on the depredations of rabbits among the Home Farm's vegetables, 'I've a shoot on the fourteenth of August.'

'Beg pardon?' Seth said.

'The directors are coming out to Beckindale for a shoot on the fourteenth – '

'But you can't do that,' Seth exclaimed.

Anstey leaned back from his desk and frowned. 'What d'you mean, I can't?'

'I . . . er . . . I meant the date . . . is not very convenient . . .'

'It's convenient to the directors,' Anstey said in a very dry tone.

'But it's . . . that's to say . . . awkward – '

'By that time,' Anstey said, 'the Glorious Twelfth will have come and gone. What's awkward about it?'

'It's . . . er . . . the local cricket derby. Difficult to get beaters.'

'Armstrong,' said Mr Anstey in a very cool tone, 'I pay you to keep down the vermin, look after the game, and arrange sport for profit. If you can't get beaters in Beckindale, you'll get them from Hotten. But you'll arrange that shoot and be there to see it goes well.'

'Yes, sir,' Seth said with an inward groan.

There was nothing for it. He would have to alter the date of the Horticultural Show. It was unthinkable that it should take place and he not be present to walk off in triumph with the prizes for at least three of the vegetable classes.

The worst of it was, Sam Pearson would think he had won the contest over whether or not the cricket match date should stand. He'd think Seth had backed down and altered his date to suit Sam.

But there were only three weeks to go, and people would need notice of the change of date.

It would all be worth it though, when he walked off with the marrow prize that Sam Pearson was expecting to win.

But Sam Pearson, too, had an urgent notice to get into the *Courier*. He had been having a terrible time drumming up a team this year; several of his regulars had been dragged off on holiday by their wives, and of those remaining, one had an arm in plaster, one had his daughter's wedding on the very day, and a third was moving house. Sam had therefore been mightily relieved when Ecky Tait, chairman of the Robblesfield Cricket Club, had approached him for a conference.

'Sitha, lad, I'm in dire straits for players this year,' he confessed.

Sam experienced a thrill of relief. Happen the Robblesfield man was going to suggest a five-a-side. Sam could just about summon that number.

Ecky, short for Hector, had a different form of combat in mind. 'What I were wondering, Sam . . . could we change it this year to a bowls match?'

'A bowls match? For the Butterworth cricket-ball?'

'I know it seems funny, but it's either that or cancel. I just can't get a team together.'

But though he made heavy weather of it, Sam had already decided to take Ecky up on his offer. He would not cancel – Seth would think he had won over the date. He had flicked through the pages of memory and realized that Beckindale could field a team of first-class bowlers. In the end, after a suitable show of reluctance, he agreed. He then drafted a notice to the *Courier* to let all men know that the Robblesfield-versus-Beckindale Cricket Match would for this occasion only be a bowls match.

In summer, Beckindale was a hive of activity. Tourists and picnickers appeared, and of these a few were interested enough to be shown round the church. The churchwardens acted as guides when they were free to do so, and it was on one of her days on duty that Annie saw Pat Merrick put her head round the church door.

'Hello, Pat – haven't seen much of you since you came back,' she welcomed her.

'Hello, Annie. I've not been in t'village much. Living just a bit outside we tend to go t'other way, towards Hotten.'

'Owt I can do for you?'

'I were looking for Mr Hinton.'

'He's had to go to Connelton today – stand-in for Mr Trudgeon, for a christening.' She paused, looking at Pat. 'Do you want to leave a message?'

'Oh, nay, I . . . it's not important.'

But it had been important enough to bring her to the church in search of him. Annie laid her hand on the girl's arm. 'Pat, I know things haven't been easy for you, and if you need any help, don't be afraid to ask.'

'We'll manage all right, thanks.' She didn't say that Jack had made the very same offer on the evening he had walked her home from the Woolpack. She would not be beholden to anyone, least of all the Sugdens. 'The less you and I see of each other, the better. Folks have enough to talk about, as it is.'

'You know I don't pay heed to gossip, Pat.'

'Oh, I'm used to it. Tom saw to that!'

Annie hesitated. 'I saw he was up before the magistrates. Drunk and disorderly. What happened?'

'Another fine,' Pat said with a sigh. 'But it's no matter to me. I'm done with him.'

'For good, you mean?'

Pat gave a little shiver. 'It's cool in here, isn't it?'

'Always cool in a church, love. Come on, let's go out into the sunshine. What did you want to see Mr Hinton about, Pat? Can't you tell me? I'll give him the message as soon as he gets back.'

'It was just that . . . I was wondering if he had heard of any places to live, any jobs going?'

'In Beckindale, you mean?'

'I can't stay with Auntie Elsie for ever,' Pat burst out, throwing out her hands in a gesture of rejection. 'She means well but . . .'

'Aye, she's not used to having children in her house, I suppose,' Annie said, catching quickly what the girl meant. She knew Elsie Harker – a quiet, plain-living Christian woman but excessively house-proud. Not the kind to take kindly to muddy boots, transistor radios, bikini panties drying in the bathroom or bikes being repaired in the kitchen.

'I've told them and told them. They should be grateful for a roof over our heads. But . . .'

'But they can't take to it. I don't blame them,' Annie said. 'Well, I'll talk to the vicar, love, and I'll keep my ears open. But I doubt there's much going around here. The cottages are mostly let out for holidays this time of year, and jobs have always been scarce.'

'I know, I've tried the Exchange in Hotten – nothing. I thought that happen the vicar might know of somebody who needs help in the house – that kind of thing.'

'He may do. We'll see what we can do, Pat.'

'Thanks, Annie. You always were a kind woman . . .' Pat nodded, turned quickly, and hastened away.

Sadly Annie watched her go. Why did life have to be so unjust? Pat was a decent lass, and from what she'd seen of the children, they were fine-looking youngsters. If only Jack hadn't left home! He might have married Pat, and those two children would have been Annie's grandchildren.

She sighed to herself. Happen one of them was. Everybody said the boy was Jack's son. As for Annie, she preferred not to make any judgements on that. She regarded Pat as a nice girl who needed help, and she would try to give it. But as to helping her find a job, it was almost impossible. Any enquiries she made would have to be very discreet, for her father was very intolerant about Pat Merrick. He wanted no contact between the Sugden family and Pat.

But luckily his attention was totally taken up with two things at the moment – the vegetables he was going to exhibit at the Horticultural Show in two weeks' time and the bowls match next Saturday. He had rounded up a team of bowls experts who now were being driven to practise every evening under his beady eye.

The dreaded day dawned. The men who were to play assembled at three o'clock in the afternoon. The opposing team turned up in two cars from Robblesfield.

From the outset it was clear it was going to be a massacre. The Robblesfield men exuded confidence, and after the first two or three woods it was easy to see why. Two of their team were playing like angels.

'By heck!' groaned Sam. 'Where did they get *them*?'

Seth Armstrong, taking a moment off from his work with the shooting party, spoke in Sam's ear. 'I've just found out where they got them,' he said. 'One of the beaters I hired in Hotten knows them two. He got 'em from the county team – Sid Allworth is the captain of the champion bowls team.'

'But that's . . . that's . . .'

'Clever footwork?' Seth suggested.

'I were going to say, it's not cricket!'

Seth made his way back to the shooting brake with a smothered grin on his face. Before the day was out, he knew, Sam would have to take the Butterworth Ball from its place of honour in the Woolpack and hand it over to Ecky Tait and the men from Robblesfield.

Sam was indignant, humiliated, and outfoxed. He vowed that next week he would show them all that Sam Pearson was not to be trifled with. He would walk off with the best prizes at the Horticultural Show.

'I wouldn't be too sure of that,' Amos said as he listened to the mutter of self-justification in the Woolpack bar that evening. '*I'm* entering in the marrow class.'

'You?' Sam said, in a tone that conveyed what he thought of Amos's chances.

'Let me tell you, Sam, I have a very fine specimen. I *told* you my method of culture was special, now didn't I?'

Sam shrugged and buried his nose in his half pint of cider. Fate might deal him many unkind blows, but the day would never dawn when Amos Brearly could beat Sam Pearson in a vegetable show.

He was right. The marrow class was won by a huge specimen, larger by every measurement than any other. It beat Sam's. It beat Amos's too. It even beat Seth's.

It was entered by Nellie Ratcliffe. 'Oh, I always have a marrow or two in my back garden,' she said blithely as she walked off with the rosette. 'They're so easy to grow, aren't they?'

What made it harder for Sam to bear was that he came joint second with Amos Brearly and Seth Armstrong. Annie had a hard time keeping her face straight at the result.

But amusement died as she sighted a figure that could only mean trouble – Tom Merrick, shouldering his way through the groups in the marquee, eyes everywhere, a glower of angry discontent on his features. It could only mean trouble – and trouble for Pat Merrick, at that.

Pat was here, having some innocent enjoyment at the Show. There were always a few amusements for the youngsters at the Horticultural Show, so it was only to be expected she would have brought Jackie and Sandie. If they came face to face with Tom, there would be a scene.

A moment's quick thought told Annie that prevention was better than cure. She left her father, still fuming over the cards on the marrow entries, and hurried through the show ground until she met the village constable. Ted Edwards always showed up at such events in his uniform. He felt it was good for public relations for the police to be on view, ready for action but also ready to chat.

When Annie approached him he thought it was just for a few kind words. But she said in a low voice, 'Ted, Pat Merrick's husband is wandering about among the exhibitors – and he looks as if he's had a few.'

'Oh dear – he generally has,' the constable agreed.

'It's just that if he's in the mood for a fight, he could spoil the day.'

'Aye, right . . . I'll see to him.'

He moved away, apparently at ease but with a certain amount of speed. It wasn't Tom Merrick he spied first, but the boy, Jackie. He was swinging enthusiastically in the swingboat set up by a local fairground operator. Edwards saw the boy's gaze go suddenly stiff, saw dismay and fear come into his eyes. He followed his glance. His father was shouldering his way towards the swingboat.

Edwards went after him. Someone got in his way, said welcomingly, 'Hello, constable, enjoying yourself?'

Tom Merrick heard. He turned his florid, heavy face and saw the policeman. A natural disinclination to have anything to do with the Law caused him to veer away from his son, whom he'd been just about to clout into submission. He set off towards the edge of the field, anxious to be out of range of the constable's arm.

Tom Merrick considered he had a justifiable grievance against Beckindale. It had given shelter to his wife and to Jack Sugden, who had made Merrick a laughing stock through that long piece in the *Sunday Gazette*. All Merrick's cronies had been joshing him about it ever since. If he'd known at the time what that reporter feller was going to do with the information, he'd never have taken that fiver from him – but too late now to withdraw his remarks, and too far to go to punch his head. Instead, he could make life a misery for his wife and children. And if it happened he came across Jack Sugden in the process, he would break his back for him.

But not with a copper looking on.

Annie saw the policeman following someone through the crowd, and went a little way after to see if it was Tom Merrick. She felt a hand on her arm. It was Jack. 'Was that Merrick I just saw?' he asked.

'Never mind, Jack. Ted Edwards will deal with him.'

Jack frowned, then walked on. Annie went at his side, her hand on his sleeve, trying to draw him back.

Tom Merrick had come to a halt beside a rather shabby old Hillman. He was fumbling in his pocket for the keys. Annie and Jack watched as the constable came to Merrick's side.

'What you want?' Merrick blurted, glaring at him out of bloodshot eyes. 'You going to breathalyze me, eh? I've only had a pint or two.'

'Or three or four.' Edwards leaned a little to one side and eyed the car. 'This yours?'

'Aye, and it's passed M.O.T. so don't try to make anything of it.'

'Oh, it has, has it?'

'You wanna see the certificate?'

'No, but I'd like to see your road fund licence, if you don't mind.'

'My . . . er . . .?'

'Because, Mr Merrick, I have to point out to you that the disc on your windscreen is dated June. And today's date is August twenty-first. I'm afraid you're driving an unlicensed vehicle, and that being so, I must warn you . . .'

Merrick gave a roar of rage and lunged at the constable. Ted sidestepped, caught his assailant by one arm, and twisted it behind him. 'Assaulting the police. That's a very grave charge, Merrick. I must ask you to come with me . . .' The rest of his words were lost as he marched Tom Merrick off, flailing and protesting, towards the police cottage.

Jack turned to his mother. 'Did you have anything to do with that, Ma?'

'Well, I'd no idea his road fund licence had run out.'

They looked at each other. Jack smiled. 'Come back to the marquee,' he invited, 'and I'll buy you a cup of tea.'

She took the arm he offered. Together they wended their way back to the Show, where Pat Merrick stood, unaware of what she had been spared, watching her children swoop up and down in the swingboat.

Chapter Eleven

Joe sought out his mother on a cold but golden-bright September morning. 'Have you a couple of minutes to spare, Ma? I need to talk to you.'

She saw that he had chosen his moment well. Dolly was at her playgroup, Matt and Jack were bringing the sheep down to the shelter of the lower slopes for autumn grazing. Her father was out in his shed working on a piece of carving for the Harvest Festival Bazaar.

'Can I go on working while we talk?' she asked, with half a smile. She was making bread; she baked bread twice a week, and always on Friday so that there would be plenty for the weekend. Her hands worked the dough with sure, strong movements while she studied her younger son. 'Well, lad?'

'Has our Jack said anything to you about how long he's staying in Beckindale this time?' he asked.

She was a little surprised. She'd thought it was something of a more personal nature he'd been about to mention – perhaps to do with Kitty Lennard, whom he sometimes visited in Sussex, or Judy. But he and Judy seemed to spend little time together these days. Both of them were taken up with their work.

'I'm not sure Jack knows himself, Joe.' She thought about it. 'I'd say he's pretty settled. He seemed . . . very deeply taken with protecting the countryside over that poisoned seed. And the pedigree cows – I think he wants to stay around and see their calves, at least.'

Joe nodded. 'But has he said anything?'

'Not to me. To Matt, happen?'

'Nay, I've asked Matt.'

She kneaded the dough for a moment in silence.

'Whatever it is that's on your mind, you'd best leave Jack out of the reckoning.'

'I don't think I can.' He sat down on a chair by the table, watching her. 'I've been offered a job.'

'I see.' Her words were cool, almost uninterested. It was surprise that brought about her distant manner. Joe, understanding this, remained silent. 'Who by?' she asked.

'N.Y. Estates. Richard Anstey has asked me to be his Farm Manager.'

She nodded. 'Shows how much he thinks of you, then.' She picked up a folded tea cloth, put it over the bowl, and set it by the hearth for the dough to rise. 'When was this?'

'About a week ago. He's been coming towards it for a while now – ever since I got back from the States, I realize now. We've talked, and he's hinted that I could do better than managing Emmerdale, and I've told him there's no prospect of owt else because I'm the only one to do it. But he said to me last night that our Jack seems to have a head on his shoulders and a will to take on the management of Emmerdale.'

'Oh aye?' she said non-committally. 'And you – what'd it be for you?'

'I'd be running the three N.Y. farms. That's over nine hundred acres, Ma.'

'Quite an undertaking.'

'Aye, and there'd be money to expand, and to use the best equipment. They're doing things we'd never do at Emmerdale.'

'Such as?'

'Oh . . . Forestry. Bigger range of arable crops. New methods of milk production. But it's the whole of their system of farming that interests me, Ma. It would be as good as going to university – I'd learn so much. They do things that we only read about.'

Annie rinsed her hands under the tap and dried them methodically. 'Sounds to me as if you've already made your mind up.'

'Nay,' he said strongly, his dark eyes fixed on her in a plea for her understanding. 'It's not as easy as that, and you know it. First off, there's who'd take on if I went. I'm asking about Jack, and if Jack were to stay happen he'd be willing to bear the brunt of it. With Henry to advise him on finance and Matt to steer him about t'livestock – and me not far off if he wanted to discuss anything other than day-to-day problems – he'd not be badly off. But there's my own point of view too. I'm my own boss here at Emmerdale. I mean, we're not likely to expand much further here, but at least we're accountable only to ourselves.'

'Aye, you've not had to kow-tow to anyone for a long time, not since your father went.'

'Besides,' Joe added, with a sigh, 'Emmerdale's *home*.'

Annie nodded. They were silent for a moment. Then she said, 'It's not as if you're going to the ends of the earth, though.'

'The thing is,' he almost broke in, 'it's a chance to have a crack at the kind of farming I saw in America. Well, some of it, any road.'

'You think you might take this job?' she asked, carefully neutral.

'I don't know.'

'When does Mr Anstey want his answer?'

'End of the month.'

'Good. Then you've time to think about it.'

Joe shook his head and rose to his feet with a sagging look to his shoulders. 'The way my mind's been going round in circles since he first made the offer, I don't see thinking's going to be much help.'

His mother picked up the kettle and went to the sink to fill it. It would soon be time for elevenses, and no matter what happened, the farm routine had to go on. She said over her shoulder, as if casually, 'I know how you feel, lad. You want someone to nudge you one way or the other. But this is a thing where you have to make up your own mind.'

'Aye.'

She set the kettle on the Aga. She stood looking at it, as if it could provide the answers. 'When you were a boy, Joe, you made up your mind to do a thing and did it without asking. I watched you do some things I thought were right daft, but I left you to it. It's the only way he'll learn, I thought.' She smiled and went to take coffee mugs from the dresser. 'Even when you were older . . .'

He knew she meant his disastrous marriage with Christine, and his flaunting of Beckindale convention by living with Kathy. 'But this is different, Ma. This is something that could concern all of us, our livelihood . . .'

'Ah, don't hide behind that,' she warned, though in a gentle voice. 'We'll never starve, not while Matt's here to see to things and I've my health and strength – not forgetting Henry and his financial advice. No, Joe, this is summat you'll have to study out for yourself. Whatever you decide, you can count on me to back you up. But I'll not make up your mind for you.'

Her son nodded. 'I know you're right. But there's one thing I'd like to ask. Where would you start, in trying to balance one thing against another?'

'It's Jack, isn't it? You can't go with an easy conscience unless you know there are at least enough pairs of hands to do the work, and preferably somebody who's ready to . . . to commit himself to it.'

'Aye,' Joe said. 'I'd best have a word with our Jack, I think.' He made for the door. 'I'll just go and do a bit of work on the supply list. Eh . . . Ma . . . don't mention this to anyone for the present, will you?'

'Of course not, lad.'

The morning took its usual course. If Joe was preoccupied, no one noticed except Annie. He went to Beckindale to discuss the harvest supper with the vicar, for Emmerdale as usual was to provide some of the food, and as he strolled back through the churchyard he came on Henry Wilks doing a bit of hedge-clipping for the vicar. 'How do, Henry. Short back and sides, eh?'

'Happen this'll be the last trim until next spring,' Henry said. 'Yew's appropriate to churchyards, of course, but it's a nuisance when it comes to trimming.' He laid the shears by. 'Joe, you still get phone calls from Ed Hathersage?'

'Not so often. He still writes, though.'

'It's true he's selling the farm, though?'

'Looks like it. His Dakota place is draining money out of him.'

'Any idea how much he wants for it?'

Joe raised his eyebrows at him. 'Thinking of making an offer for it?'

'If I don't, someone else will. The house is a big attraction.'

'Nine months' neglect since he died, and the attentions of the holiday vandals . . . you're welcome to it, Henry. What are you thinking of doing with the place? Renting it to Dolly and Matt?'

'Nay, I still think this museum idea could work. But if we muck along trying to get committees together, we'll never get anywhere.' Henry leaned back against a convenient gravestone for a rest. 'Unless we make a determined effort, we'll never get it off the ground.'

Joe laughed. 'So it's going to be the Henry Wilks Memorial Museum, not the Hathersage?'

'Don't laugh, Joe. I just want a proper museum properly set up and run.'

'Who's going to farm it?'

'We can sort that out later. The first thing is to see if we can raise the money.'

'You wouldn't think of adding it to Emmerdale?' Joe enquired, edging towards a discussion that he wanted.

'Nay, Emmerdale couldn't afford it. When I speak of raising money, I mean public money. A pity, of course, because Emmerdale could use the land . . .'

Joe took his opportunity. 'Wouldn't you say we've gone about as far as we can go? Without expanding, I mean – and you've just said there's no hope of that.'

'I don't think we can envisage expansion. The best we can do for the next, say, ten years is to work it as efficiently as a farm our size can be worked.'

'Hm,' said Joe. 'Emmerdale is already supporting six people – or five and a half if we regard your income as gained mostly from t'Woolpack. What's to happen if I want to get married again, or Jack gets married – or Matt and Dolly start the family they want so much?'

Henry grinned. 'Books not balancing?' he enquired with sympathy.

'That's not what I'm talking about,' Joe said, refusing to let it go by as a joke. 'You're looking for a challenge over this museum, Henry. Maybe I'm looking for something with a bit more challenge to it too.'

'You've still got your head full of Yankee ideas,' Henry jeered. 'Come down to earth, lad.'

'You agree it's no go for bigger things at Emmerdale?'

'Bigger isn't necessarily better, Joe.'

'But it would be interesting to find out . . .' Joe moved away. 'Up shears and at 'em,' he commanded as he made for the gate.

Henry picked up his tool and clipped a few twigs of yew. Then he paused to look after Joe. He was hearing overtones in the conversation now. But it was too late to try to resume it.

Late that night Annie was knitting by the fire while Jack finished looking through the *Courier*. Sam had gone up to bed, Matt and Dolly were out for an evening in Leeds.

'Good lord,' Jack said, 'Caroline Tanner's got herself married. Remember her?'

'Of course I do. Who has she married?'

'Oh . . . some accountant from Hotten.' He folded the paper and put it by. 'Reckon Joe will ever get married again?'

'What makes you ask that?' his mother replied, with a faint frown.

'He's got a lot of lady friends.'

'Joe's not the only one,' Annie said. She finished a row, and put her knitting in its hold-all. 'Time for cocoa. You having some?'

'Aye, I'd love some.'

She busied herself with pouring milk into a saucepan. 'Not many mothers have two full-grown sons living at home.'

'You can't say Joe's at home – '

'Home for most meals. It feels as if he's at home, any road.'

'Is it a blessing or a bore?' he teased.

'I'm happy with it – while it lasts.'

'I'm not going anywhere, if that's what you mean.'
'Not Rome?'
'That's all gone by, Ma.'
'Joe's not the only one who might think of marriage – '
'Can't see much chance of that,' Jack said. 'For me, I mean.'
'Is it . . .' She wanted to ask, 'Is it Pat or no one?' But she never liked to pry.
'There isn't anybody, Ma,' Jack said, very matter of fact. 'Just as well, because I want to give my full attention to the farm so I get the hang of it.'
'I see.' She decided to take it just a little further. 'Are you speaking of it as a permanent thing?'
'Permanent as anything is in this changing world, Ma.' He was smiling, totally unaware of the importance she set on his words.

Next morning, after milking, the men dispersed about various tasks. Matt went up to the pastures to check that the grass was still sufficient for the sheep. Jack went to fetch in the barley straw. Joe worked on a couple of old felled trees, cutting them into lengths for the fire. The chainsaw packed up when he restarted it after hitting a snag. He was still fiddling with it when Jack came back on the tractor and trailer.
'Can't get it to go,' Joe called.
'You've flooded it,' Jack replied. 'I can smell the fuel.'
'Aye, you're right, I s'pose.' He laid it down and came to watch Jack back the trailer up to the doors of the barn. 'Jack listen . . .'
'Aye?'
'You've been back since May. I were just wondering how long you're going to stay.'
His brother turned in the tractor seat to stare at him. 'Why?'
'Just wanted to know, that's all.'
There was a silence while Jack opened the door of the tractor cab, jumped down, and turned to look at Joe. 'You must have a reason. Have I outstayed my welcome?'

'Nay, don't take it like that. I was thinking about the farm – how we're going to run it. When you first arrived there was no way of knowing whether you were staying six weeks or six months. Ma said not to bother you. And any road, this is your home, you've a right.'

Jack was frowning. 'I thought I was fitting in pretty well.'

'You're right. We've been glad of your help, and grateful for the contribution to the pedigree herd. Only you can't run a business not knowing what's the state of play. You've got to make plans, haven't you? And that means you've got to be sure who you can count on.'

His brother moved restlessly, put his hands in his pockets, leaned back against the tractor wheel. 'Whether I stay or go might depend on what those plans are.'

Joe sighed inwardly. It was always difficult to have a conversation with Jack. He was reticent to the point of being secretive; it was as if he feared to reveal any of his inner thoughts.

'No point beating about the bush,' said Joe. 'Anstey's offered me the job as his Farm Manager.'

Whatever Jack had been expecting, it wasn't that. He was absolutely taken aback. His first reaction was to say, 'What, you?' because to some extent he still regarded Joe as his kid brother. But the next moment he saw how right it was that Joe, who had given his whole life to farming, should be offered a reward like that.

'I haven't decided whether I'll take it yet or not,' Joe went on in a brisk manner, 'but if I do . . .'

'I see what you mean.'

'Well?'

'Well what?'

'Ah, come on, Jack. If you stay and work the farm, my decision is easier. If you decide to up stumps again, I have to turn the job down.'

'You mean if I say I'm leaving, you'll feel duty bound to stay here.'

Joe was vexed. His brother was turning his words round. 'I'm not trying to put it on to you, to make it possible one way or the other. I just want to *know* what you intend doing.'

They faced each other, so alike in their dark good looks, yet not quite friends and allies. 'Do I have to make a lifelong commitment just this minute?'

'You must know your own mind, Jack.'

'I know how I feel at this moment. How do I know how I'll feel in six months? It's no good, Joe. In six months, if you take Anstey's job, you may see you've made a mistake and want to come back.'

'It's not likely. Since I went to America I've realized I need an education in modern farming. This job's one way of getting it.'

Jack shrugged and turned to start heaving straw bales out of the tractor trailer. 'Strikes me you've made up your mind already,' he said.

'If I had, what would you say?'

'I wouldn't say anything,' Jack said, shouldering a bale. 'I'm out of breath, working.'

Joe turned away and restarted the chainsaw. It was always the same when he tried to have a conversation with Jack – like trying to trap the beck in your fingers.

Richard Anstey wasn't content to let matters rest. He wanted Joe Sugden to take on the post that was vacant on N.Y. Estates, and he wanted the decision to be made before his board of directors started asking why he didn't advertise the post. 'Let me show you round a bit,' he said to Joe a few days later. 'You want to see the kind of thing you'd be getting into.'

It turned into a guided tour that took most of the following afternoon, and it was an eye-opener. Anstey picked Joe up in a new Japanese four-wheel drive, so that they could go over any kind of terrain. They paused at a new construction site, where a silo was going up. In a long shed nearby, farming vehicles were parked, some of them under neat tarpaulins. As they drove from there towards the woodlands Joe saw a big digger taking out old hedges. 'I know what you're going to say,' Anstey remarked as Joe opened his mouth. 'I've had it all from Seth Armstrong. But the fields aren't big enough for proper use of our combines so they have to go.'

'Seth hates to see hedges grubbed up –

'He's got plenty to think about otherwise. We're making quite a thing of the game crop, you know. And money comes in from the shoots.'

The woodlands were new to Joe, in their present form. He saw that N.Y. Estates had taken out a lot of scrub oak and hawthorn, to replace it with more useful saplings. 'A long term crop,' Anstey said, with a wave of his arm, 'but profitable.'

So it went on. As they drove back to the Home Farm, Joe began to think he would hate to lose the chance of managing all this.

'Home Farm has one of the most up-to-date milking systems,' Anstey said. 'Ridge Farm still needs some modernization and we're going to make some changes at Raventop next year. Thought you'd like to take charge of all that, get in at the beginning, you see.'

'It's a great scheme.'

'I hope it gave you a sort of oversight of the whole project. What do you think?'

'About what?'

'Will you be taking up my offer?'

'I . . . er . . . didn't know you'd want a decision today?'

'No, not essentially. But do you feel you'd like to come?'

'It's hard to resist,' Joe sighed. 'I'll let you know in a day or two.'

'I'll look forward to your answer,' said Anstey, eyeing him with his keen, dark gaze.

There was another stage in the decision making. Joe had to talk to Matt about it. Matt had been his closest friend and confidant for years, so he knew that from him he could expect some helpful comments. He sought him out when he was just back from Hotten Market, flushed with pleasure at the prices he and Jack had got for their lambs.

'Jack's not bad at doing person-to-person deals,' he reported. 'He stands there looking . . . what d'you call it – inscrutable. And they up the price a bit.'

'He's got a lot of hidden talent,' Joe said. 'I never thought he'd stick it this long.'

Matt thought about that. 'I s'pose I didn't, either. But now I take it for granted he's staying.'

'For how long?'

'Well, for ever, more or less.'

'Has he ever actually said that to you?'

'I don't recall,' Matt said. 'Why?'

'Because I'm thinking of leaving Emmerdale, Matt.'

Matt was putting receipts for the lambs in the record book. He paused, looked round at Joe. 'You what?'

'I've been offered the job of Farm Manager for N.Y. Estates.'

There was a little silence. Then Matt said, 'Well, good for you. They're showing sense, I see.'

'Thanks, Matt. I was a bit chuffed myself, at getting the offer. I mean, they approached me, not t'other way about. But the thing is, I can't go if Jack isn't staying.'

'You want to go?' Matt asked. And then, 'Aye, I can see you do.'

'It's not that I want to leave Emmerdale. But this is . . . you know . . . an offer I can't refuse. Unless Jack pushes off again. I couldn't leave you with the whole thing on your hands, Matt.'

'No, that'd be bad,' Matt agreed, without attempting to puff himself up by saying he'd manage. 'I'm not good on the managerial thing. But I don't reckon Jack's going anywhere.'

'Have you any reason for saying that?'

'He's sort of . . . worked himself into it. And another thing. He doesn't say owt, but I think Pat Merrick is important to him.'

'You mean he wouldn't leave because of her?'

'If she stays, Jack will stay, I think. And I don't think she's got anywhere else to go, so she'll stay.'

'Would you think it wrong if I took the job? Left Emmerdale?'

Matt clapped him on the shoulder. 'Get on wi' thee! What's wrong in taking a step up in your career? You've given a good many years to Emmerdale, some of 'em right hard ones. You deserve what you can get, lad.'

Joe decided to make one more try with his brother. He couldn't exactly say to him that he was being selfish in refusing to give a definite answer when he himself was preparing to walk away from the farm, but he thought over one or two phrases that might imply it.

But in fact he never used them. Matt and Jack did the evening milking, and then over the evening meal Jack entertained them all with an account of his selling the lambs in Hotten Market. Dolly was in gales of laughter, Annie smiled and shook her head at him, even Sam chuckled from time to time although Jack had been pulling a fast one over his purchaser.

Joe was content to listen and observe. His brother was so entirely at home here, so pleased with life and with himself – it was impossible to believe he would suddenly pack and leave. Although Jack was unpredictable, the odds seemed stacked against his getting tired of Beckindale.

That evening in the Woolpack Joe had further evidence that Jack was likely to find something worth staying for in Beckindale. Pat Merrick came into the pub, shyly but as if she was expected. She caught Jack's eye and went to join him at a table by the fire. Jack bought her a drink, and soon they were deep in conversation, their heads close together.

Matt had said, 'Pat Merrick is important to him.' True, Pat was the wife of another man. But that didn't mean there couldn't be a strong bond between her and Jack, strong enough to tie Jack to Emmerdale for at least the foreseeable future.

After all, Joe said to himself, nothing's for ever. Even if I take this job, I suppose I won't stay there for the rest of my life. All I need is to think of the foreseeable future.

He waited until the Woolpack was almost closing. Then he said to Henry, 'Can I have a word with you when everybody's gone?'

Henry looked surprised at the quiet tone of voice. 'Summat up?'

'I'll tell you later.'

The pub cleared slowly. Amos glared at Joe when he showed no signs of leaving but shrugged when Henry invited him into the back room. Farm business, he supposed. He made cocoa for all three, then took his upstairs to have as a bedside drink. 'Good night, Mr Wilks. Don't forget to lock up properly when Joe leaves.'

'I won't forget, Amos. Good night.'

They heard his footsteps go upstairs and his door close. Then Henry looked at Joe. 'This is something serious,' he said.

'Serious enough, Henry. I'm taking a job with N.Y. Estates as their Farm Manager.'

Henry was surprised, but not quite as surprised as Matt. Something in the talk he'd had with Joe in the churchyard had alerted him. 'I see,' he said slowly. 'Well done, lad. That's a big step up.'

'I wouldn't take it just for the money, though that's good. It's the chance to learn, Henry. I've felt since I got back to Beckindale from the States that everything here is almost standing still. I want to be going forward, with the new ideas in farming.'

'I understand. What happens about managing Emmerdale?'

'I'm hoping you'll go on handling the financial side. I've decided that Jack's either got to put his shoulder to the wheel, or say he won't. But I believe he'll go along with my decision. He's settled at Emmerdale for the time being. And of course there's always Matt – like the Rock of Gibraltar, is Matt. Jack can't go far wrong if he's got you and Matt. And I'll be nearby if I'm needed.'

Henry held out his hand. 'Well, good luck to you, lad,' he said, shaking. 'I'd do the same if I were your age. Have you told your family?'

'No. Not yet. I'm going to tell them tomorrow morning. I wanted to tell you first and then speak about it as a settled thing.'

'Annie isn't expecting this?'

'I think she is,' Joe said. 'But it won't be much fun, anyhow.'

He dreaded it. He had a terrible feeling his brother would shy away at the prospect of the added responsibility. So he slept badly that night at Demdyke, and was silent all through milking with Jack and Matt.

At breakfast, when the first edge of appetite had been appeased, Joe glanced round the table. Surprisingly, a silence fell. Sam Pearson looked about him. What was the matter with them all?

'I've something to tell you,' Joe said.

'What?' said his grandfather.

'I've been offered a new job.' Then, to the rest of his family, 'I've accepted the offer of the job as Farm Manager of N.Y. Estates.'

Sam was staggered. 'You're going to work for Mr Anstey?' he demanded, in disbelief.

'Congratulations,' said Dolly.

'Well done,' Matt said.

Annie smiled and nodded at him.

Joe was watching his brother. 'He wants me to start as soon as we get things sorted out here,' he said.

Jack met his eyes. 'That should be easy enough, shouldn't it?' he queried. He rose and held out his hand. 'Well done, brother,' he said.

A great burden seemed to slip off Joe's back. Jack was saying he would stay.

He glanced at his mother. She was looking from one to the other with something like pride.

It was going to be all right. He could leave, in the knowledge that Emmerdale was in good hands. The future lay ahead with a new world waiting for him.

Winston Graham

'One of the best half-dozen novelists in this country.' *Books and Bookmen*.

'Winston Graham excels in making his characters come vividly alive.' *Daily Mirror*.

'A born novelist.' *Sunday Times*.

The Poldark Saga, his famous story of eighteenth-century Cornwall

ROSS POLDARK
DEMELZA
JEREMY POLDARK
WARLEGGAN
THE BLACK MOON
THE FOUR SWANS
THE ANGRY TIDE
THE STRANGER FROM THE SEA
THE MILLER'S DANCE
THE LOVING CUP

His immensely popular suspense novels include

THE WALKING STICK
MARNIE
THE SLEEPING PARTNER

Historical novel

THE FORGOTTEN STORY

Taylor Caldwell

One of today's best-selling authors, Taylor Caldwell has created a host of unforgettable characters in her novels of love, hate, drama and intrigue, set against rich period backgrounds.

'Taylor Caldwell is a born storyteller.'

Chicago Tribune

THE BEAUTIFUL IS VANISHED
CAPTAINS AND THE KINGS
TESTIMONY OF TWO MEN
THE EAGLES GATHER
THE FINAL HOUR
THIS SIDE OF INNOCENCE
DYNASTY OF DEATH
CEREMONY OF THE INNOCENT